SUDDEN FEAR

Myra Hudson is t͟h͟e͟ ͟l͟a͟s͟t͟ ͟o͟f͟ ͟t͟h͟e͟ Hudsons, and her fame, wealth and power are legendary. She has written seven plays in the last fifteen years, all of them successful. Now she watches the rehearsal for her latest, "Immoral Courage," and notices that one of the male leads, Lester Blaine, is too handsome for the part. So she has him removed. But there he is on opening night, charming his way past her defenses—and into her life.

Their subsequent marriage seems perfect. Lester is the ideal husband, devoted and attentive. Then one day while listening back to last night's Dictaphone recordings Myra discovers a horrible secret. The machine had been activated when Lester and Irma Neves, Myra's protégé, had entered the room later that night—and secretly made plans to kill her.

Edna Sherry Bibliography
(1885-1967)

Novels:

Is No One Innocent? (1930; with Milton Herbert Gropper,
   based on their play, *Inspector Kennedy*)
Grounds for Indecency (1931; with Milton Herbert Gropper)
Sudden Fear (1948)
No Questions Asked (1949)
Backfire (1956; reprinted in paperback as *Murder at Nightfall*)
Tears for Jessie Hewitt (1958; reprinted in paperback as *She Asked for
   Murder*)
The Defense Does Not Rest (1959)
The Survival of the Fittest (1960)
Call the Witness (1961)
Girl Missing (1962)
Strictly a Loser (1965)

Short Stories:

The Crimson Girl (with Charles K. Harris; *Munsey's Magazine*, March 1927)
Strange Cargo (with Charles K. Harris; *Sweetheart Stories*, Jan 24 1928)

Plays:

Guilty? (1923)
Inspector Kennedy (aka *Homicide*, 1929; with Milton Hernert Gropper)
We Are as We Are (1934; with Emma Mandel)

Film Scripts:

Through Different Eyes (1929; with Milton Herbery Gropper)

Sudden Fear
••••••••••••••••
Edna Sherry

Introduction by Curtis Evans

Stark House Press • Eureka California

SUDDEN FEAR

Published by Stark House Press
1315 H Street
Eureka, CA 95501, USA
griffinskye3@sbcglobal.net
www.starkhousepress.com

SUDDEN FEAR
Originally published by Dodd, Mead & Company, New York, and
copyright © 1948 by Edna Sherry.

Reprinted by arrangement with agent. All rights reserved under
International and Pan-American Copyright Conventions.

"Sudden Fame: Edna Sherry's Sudden Fear" © 2023 by Curtis Evans

ISBN: 979-8-88601-035-0

Text and cover design by Mark Shepard, shepgraphics.com
Proofreading by Bill Kelly

PUBLISHER'S NOTE:
This is a work of fiction. Names, characters, places and incidents are
either the products of the author's imagination or used fictionally, and
any resemblance to actual persons, living or dead, events or locales, is
entirely coincidental.
Without limiting the rights under copyright reserved above, no part of
this publication may be reproduced, stored, or introduced into a retrieval
system or transmitted in any form or by any means (electronic,
mechanical, photocopying, recording or otherwise) without the prior
written permission of both the copyright owner and the above publisher
of the book.

First Stark House Press Edition: August 2023

7

Sudden Fame
Edna Sherry's *Sudden Fear*
by Curtis Evans

21

Sudden Fear
byEdna Sherry

Sudden Fame
Edna Sherry's *Sudden Fear*

by Curtis Evans

When Edna Sherry's crime novel *Sudden Fear*—a gripping domestic triangle tale about a wealthy but plain New York woman playwright who discovers to her mortification that her strikingly handsome, younger husband and his beautiful, clandestine paramour are planning to murder her—was published the eminent Red Badge Detective mystery fiction imprint of Dodd, Mead and Company in the United States in February 1948, its author was a wealthy, sixty-two year old New York matron, who herself had begun writing mystery plays for the stage a quarter of a century earlier. Authors proverbially are urged to write what they know, and with *Sudden Fear*—a story about a New York playwright embroiled in real life murder—Edna Sherry emphatically did so with smashing success, producing one of the best reviewed crime novels of 1948. Four years later it enjoyed even greater acclaim in its incarnation as the multi-Oscar nominated suspense film of the same title, starring Joan Crawford, Jack Palance and Gloria Grahame. In her later years as a crime novelist Edna Sherry achieved sudden national fame on a grand scale that had largely eluded her earlier in her life (despite some successes), when she had been a playwright of murder.

Doubtlessly inspired by the massive stage success of *The Bat* (1920) and *The Cat and the Canary* (1922), Broadway smashes that were adapted as films multiple times over the years, Edna Sherry—who had been born Edna Solomon in Cincinnati, Ohio in 1885, the daughter of an affluent haberdasher, and had graduated from Hunter College (then Normal College of the

City of New York) with a degree in English in 1906, winning the Bernard Cohen Prize of $40 (around $1300 today) for best English composition—made her first stab at literary fame with her own mystery play in 1923, which she queryingly entitled *Guilty?* Although a critic praised the ingenuity of its plotting, the play died a quick death in Baltimore, due, to a great extent, to a rather unlucky break that occurred when the production's electrician repeatedly turned on the lights while the hands were still on stage shifting scenes, inducing from the audience "roars of laughter" as startled men rushed "for elusive exits."

Edna scored her first real literary successes a half-dozen years later in collaboration with Milton Herbert Gropper, a handsome playwright and screenwriter of Rumanian Jewish derivation who, although a decade younger than Edna, had already had a half-dozen plays performed on Broadway, including the provocatively-titled hit *Ladies of the Evening* (1924), which was adapted by director Frank Capra as the hit 1930 film *Ladies of Leisure*, starring a youthful Barbara Stanwyck. The first of the creative duo's collaborative successes—Milton is credited with dialogue and Edna with the story—was the film *Through Different Eyes*, a courtroom murder melodrama innovatively told in a series of flashbacks from multiple perspectives, in anticipation of the great 1950 Japanese film *Rashomon*. Milton's and Edna's *Eyes*, which was originally available in both silent and newfangled talking versions (regrettably the "talkie" version since has been lost) and marked the first significant film appearance of actress Sylvia Sidney, was well-received by reviewers. In a long, laudatory notice in the *New York Times*, for example, film critic Mordaunt Hall praised *Eyes* as an "ingeniously conceived murder trial story, one that lends itself to three different shadings of the leading characters."

Later that year Milton's and Edna's locked-room mystery play *Inspector Kennedy* (also known as *Homicide*) premiered on Broadway at the Bijou Theater. Although the play, which was packed to its melodramatic rafters with "a police inspector and a number of detectives, a leader of a dope ring, secret panels, a couple of mysterious murders and [several] men and women with motives that might have prompted them to commit the crimes," ran at the Bijou for only forty-three performances between December 20, 1929 and January 25, 1930, it was successfully taken on the road, with productions staged in Boston, Chicago, Detroit, Pittsburgh, Wilmington, Delaware and Windsor, Ontario, among other locales. The title role of Inspector Kennedy was played, in his penultimate performance before his retirement, by hugely popular "road" actor William Hodge, who also directed the play. Of Hodge the *New York Times* noted, at his death in 1932: "'The William Hodge public' was a Broadway phrase meaning that whether or not the Hodge plays were successful in New York ... he could be sure of a keen response almost anywhere in the country."

Striking while the bloody poker was hot, Milton and Edna novelized the play in 1930 under the catchy querulous title *Is No One Innocent?* However, the next year the pair followed this novelization with a would-be spicy melodrama, *Grounds for Indecency*, which was issued by what crime writer Bill Pronzini characterizes as a "schlock publisher": The Macaulay Company, which "specialized in what passed for sex novels in the flapper era." The book quickly faded away into the ether of earnest failures. Aside from her three-act comedy *We Are as We Are*, (co-authored with Emma Mandel), which saw performance in Sharon, CT, where the Sherrys owned a summer place, Edna's creative well seems to have run dry. Indeed, her literary name faded so completely during the Thirties and Forties that when *Sudden Fear* was published in 1948, many of the crime novel's reviewers assumed she was a neophyte author.

How to explain, then, the sudden success of *Sudden Fear*? In my view, the answer is simple enough: the novel is a triumph of plotting, combining the ingenuity of a Freeman Wills Crofts inverted crime novel with the credible characterization and emotional motivation of mid-century domestic suspense.

After an opening chapter where the omniscient narrator wryly ponders, as pertains to murder, *"What holds us back? Why aren't there as many murders in the average household as on the average bookshelf?,"* before concluding, *"Murder is a tough* chore," the murder tale of Myra Hudson twistingly unfolds. Independently wealthy Myra, "last in the long line of 'the' Hudsons," is also a brilliantly successful, acclaimed playwright, "important socially and financially" in New York. Attending a rehearsal of her latest play, *Immoral Courage*, she decides to can bodacious, blond Lester Blaine, who has the minor part of the play's handsome juvenile, on the seemingly perverse grounds that he is too good-looking for the role. "Overpowering," complains Myra. "He takes all the shine out of the leading lady." Ironically, however, Myra, herself a lover of youth and beauty, ends up dating and then marrying this actor she dismissed as a "male doll." ("The truth was, she wanted to go on looking at him.") Myra's society friends, including her trio of admiring male besties (Edgar Van Roon, the well-known society physician; Miles Street, custodian of the twelve-million-dollar Hudson estate; and Steve Thatcher, famed defense attorney), are initially dubious, but they are soon won over by Les' palpable dependence and devotion, where Myra is concerned, despite the fact that the "undeniably plain" Myra's greatest personal asset is her "almost masculine brain."

However, during a weekend with Les at her beach cottage at the hamlet of Manhasset on Long Island, Myra rescues a beautiful blonde nymph drowning in the breakers off the beach, a local girl named Irma Neves (daughter of the lately deceased dentist and "village drunk"), whom she promptly takes up as a sort of pet project, dazzled by her beauty and fascinated by her coolly unprincipled personality. "[S]he would squeeze her dry and put the juice into a play," thinks Myra frankly to herself. Of course the playwright is playing with fire and she soon is in grave danger of getting fatally burned, as she learns to her dismay when she overhears Les and Irma plotting her unnatural demise. Enraged and arrogantly loath to subject herself to public humiliation as an aging, betrayed wife, Myra resolves that, rather than go to the police, she will take care of the devious duo herself, doing unto them as they are plotting to do unto her.

Crime fiction reviewers were titillated with what seemed a pleasingly original innovation on the standard husband-plots-to-kill-wife theme so familiar to jaded fans of mystery in books and on stage, radio, television and film. Sometimes, as in Francis Iles' classic suspense novel *Before the Fact* (1932) (filmed by Alfred Hitchcock in 1941 under the title *Suspicion*), a wife learns her husband is trying to kill her, but she meekly spends the rest of the story trying to evade destruction, rather than boldly raining down doom upon her own would-be destroyers. Myra Hudson was something refreshingly different and reviewers applauded like they occupied box seats at one of her smash plays. Rarely has a supposed debut crime novel been received with such acclaim, with reviewers seemingly vying among themselves to provide the book with pithy praise:

"I unhesitatingly pronounce *Sudden Fear*... the best mystery novel which has come forth from a publishing house in the past year or more....Don't start reading if you have an appointment for the coming three hours or so, because you will miss the appointment. It is a one-sitting book—one that you will not put down until you have finished the last chapter, the last paragraph."—E. D. Lambright, *Tampa Tribune*

"You'll race through the pages [of *Sudden Fear*], the suspense is that terrific."—crime writer Dorothy B. Hughes, *Albuquerque Tribune*

"[*Sudden Fear*] packs a wallop that will haunt you."
—Avis De Voto, *Boston Globe*

"[I]t really is a book to be read at one sitting. It kept our light burning beyond a reasonable hour."
—Emilie Keyes, *Palm Beach Post*

"This is high-grade, edge-of-the-chair stuff, far above the general run, with most of the qualities of a real novel. Better read it."
—W. L. Knickmeyer, *Oklahoma City Daily Oklahoman*

"[A] magnificent, gripping novel of suspense....Every page is full of drama, and fear is built up so beautifully that the reader will be unable to put the book down until the last page is turned.—Richard A. Thornburgh, *Philadelphia Inquirer*

"What would you do if the playback of a Dictaphone record

revealed a plot to murder you?....Myra develops the most important plot of her career—a plot to save her own life while taking...personal revenge....This duel with death is grim fare—and a way-above-average thriller.
—Miriam Ottenberg, *Washington Evening Star*

"Edna Sherry has contrived a thriller shot through with suspense, interesting characterizations, amazing but plausible situations and a smashing climax."—*South Bend Tribune*

"[G]rips the heart of the reader and does not relinquish it until long after the story has been completed."
—*Louisville Courier-Journal*

"About all that could induce any reader to put this story down would be the outbreak of fire in the same part of the room."
—*St. Louis Post-Dispatch*

In her notice of the novel Emilie Keyes speculated that *Sudden Fear* "should make an excellent movie" and went so far as to make casting suggestions for the three main parts: "Bette Davis as the playwright; Robert Cummings as the husband; Lizabeth Scott as the other woman." Forty-year-old Bette Davis indeed would seem to have been a natural choice at the time for the part of Myra Hudson, and one could imagine twenty-six-year-old Lizabeth Scott, who would appear the next year as the fatal blonde in the classic noir *Too Late for Tears* (1949), playing Irma. However, Bob Cummings, himself pushing forty years of age with amiable but rather bland good looks, strikes me as a miss for the twenty-seven-year-old Les, a "young, graceful, beautiful creature" with a classical "Greek puss," as he self-deprecatingly puts it to Myra. This is all academic, however, for in the event none of these casting suggestions ever came to pass.

With such a superb raft of accolades, it seemed inevitable that *Sudden Fear* would indeed be filmed—and so it was. In November 1949 the *Los Angeles Times* reported that Joe Kaufman Productions had snapped up the film rights to *Sudden Fear* for the sum of $62,500, or some $710,000 today. By July 1950 Joseph Kaufman, an independent producer who had gotten his start with the Poverty Row Monogram Pictures, was said to be looking to sign fifty-one-year-old Gloria Swanson, who had recently completed filming her unforgettable man-eating role as Norma Desmond in *Sunset Boulevard*, as Myra and twenty-eight-year-old Ava Gardner as Irma. However, plans seem to have stalled for the rest of the year, while Kaufman's romantic fantasy film *Pandora and the Flying Dutchman* (which starred Gardner along with James Mason) completed filming.

Finally, nearly a year later, in June 1951, Louella Parsons divulged the exciting news that not only had forty-five-year-old Joan Crawford signed on to *Sudden Fear* to play Myra, but that she would, in a first for her, co-produce the film with Joe Kaufman, receiving, in lieu of salary, a percentage of the film's profits. As the story was given to Parsons, Crawford had read *Sudden Fear* in 1950 "and decided she'd like to do it," only to discover that Kaufman now owned the film rights. After meeting, the veteran actress and the producer struck their deal, which eventually would yield stupendous results.

In July newspapers reported that Crawford had settled on Gig Young as her leading man. At age thirty-seven, Young was actually not very young and, though handsome, no possessor of a "Greek puss," making him another miscall, seemingly, for the part of Les. However, this casting attempt fell through, leaving the role open once again. By December, even as the film was scheduled to start shooting the next month, an actor still had not been signed for the part, though Louella Parsons confided to her readers: "John Ireland [38)] would like the role and Richard Green [33] says he'd give his right arm to play it." (One has a hard-time envisioning a one-armed Les fatally charming Myra.)

Meanwhile twenty-eight-year-old blonde bombshell Jean Wallace, recently embroiled in a salacious divorce scandal with older actor Franchot Tone (who also had once been married to Joan Crawford), was bounced from the role of Irma. Twenty-eight-year-old Gloria Grahame, off her fine turn with Humphrey Bogart in the noir classic *In a Lonely Place* (1950), ended up with the role, in a perfect piece of casting. Grahame may not have been as classically beautiful as the Irma of the novel, but she caught the character's mercenary attitudes to a "T," etching a vivid "scheming vixen" image in the minds of filmgoers that has lasted up until this day.

At the famed Beverly Hills restaurant Romanoff's with *LA Times* journalist John L. Scott in December, Joan Crawford chatted about her own involvement with the film project, after "a short recital of woes with her household of four children, maids, secretary, etc." Between bites of eggs Benedict Crawford confided: "I finally found a perfectly wonderful combination of romance and suspense. During a vacation at Carmel, where I did nothing but sleep, eat and read, I went over dozens of submitted scripts—all mediocre or worse. Then I found [the novel] 'Sudden Fear' and I realized at once that it must be for me. I couldn't put that story down until I finished it." She added, with mock (?) stoicism: "I am expecting no return from 'Sudden Fear' until 1953... so I'll have to keep working on the side to feed my four kids."

Yet there was still the vexing matter of casting a leading man. Some Crawford biographies claim that at Crawford's insistence Clark Gable was offered the part of Les, but this would have been a woeful piece of miscasting, if true. (Among other things Gable was past fifty.) Louella Parsons again got the surprising scoop, however, which came in the first week of January. Les now was to be played by thirty-two-year-old Jack Palance, an actor whose skull-like visage, with its sharp, high cheekbones and deep-set eyes, was about as far-removed from a classic "Greek puss" as imaginable. Pennsylvania newspapers were particularly thrilled to report the news of a humble home state boy—the son of a native Ukrainian coal miner who boxed and played college football before entering World War Two—making good in the film world. Joan Crawford insisted that she, Joe Kaufman and director David Miller had wanted Palance "all the time," but the truth seems to have been rather more complicated, as was often the case with Crawford's self-serving pronouncements. According to Robert J. Lentz in *Gloria Grahame: Bad Girl of Film Noir* (2011), Crawford had vehemently objected to Palance as "too ugly to play her leading man," turning Myra Hudson's objection to Lester Blaine on its head. However, the director, impressed with Palance's intense performance as the lead villain in his debut film, the gripping, Elia Kazan directed thriller *Panic in the Streets*, convinced Crawford that the Pennsylvanian had the chops to stand up to and credibly menace the formidable Myra.

Indeed, Jack Palance's Les is an altogether tougher proposition than the book's beautiful blond male cipher, whom Myra, after learning of his treachery with Irma, contemptuously dismisses as nothing more than "an insect, a cockroach to be exterminated by the scuff of a shoe." (It is Irma who really frightens Myra.) Yet Palance's Les also possesses an ingratiating surface charm and a superb, athletic figure that could easily attract a woman of discernment at the dangerous age. Ironically, Crawford is said to have become so smitten with Palance during the filming of *Sudden Fear* that she wanted to become sexually involved with him, only to find out that he was already making the rounds of acquaintance, as it were, with Gloria Grahame! The older, Golden Age film star, who had something of the same temperament as the book's Myra Hudson, thereupon vengefully had Grahame exiled from the set, allowing her to appear only when she was filming one of her own scenes.

Whatever Crawford's failings as a person may have been, she undeniably had helped assemble a tremendously talented creative team and *Sudden Fear* became a substantial critical and commercial hit. The well-acted, smartly scripted, beautifully shot, evocatively scored and superbly suspenseful film was directed, as mentioned above, by David Miller, who would later helm another popular woman-in-peril thriller, *Midnight Lace* (1960), starring Doris Day and Rex Harrison; photographed (in gorgeous black and white) by Oscar-winning cinematographer Charles Lang, who shot such thriller classics as *The Cat and the Canary* (1939), *The Ghost Breakers* (1940), *The Uninvited* (1944), *Charade* (1963) and *Wait Until Dark* (1967); co-scripted by Oscar-nominated screenwriter Lenore Coffee, who back in 1929 had written the talking film adaptation of S. S. Van Dine's bestselling Philo Vance mystery *The Bishop Murder Case*, starring Basil Rathbone; and scored, in just his third filmic outing, by a young Elmer Bernstein, himself a future Oscar winner.

Rarely has a mystery writer enjoyed such a felicitous translation of her work onto film as did Edna Sherry with *Sudden Fear*. To be sure, the film softens Myra's character, making her more sympathetic, to the point where some of her actions make more immediate sense in the book than in the film (and the ending is drastically altered). Doubtlessly Crawford's ego demanded that Myra be put under a kinder light in the film than she is in the novel. Yet the translation from book to film on the whole succeeds marvelously.

The film is set primarily—and quite atmospherically—in San Francisco, rather than New York, and Les (whom Myra in contrast with the novel, gets fired from her play for *not being handsome enough*) persuasively romances the playwright (herself no longer plain in appearance) on an evocatively shot transatlantic train journey between the two cities. When Gloria Grahame's Irma brassily makes her entrance a half-hour into the film, the suspense level immediately ascends; and, after Myra learns via her Dictaphone of Les' and Irma's deadly deception, the tension does not let up for a minute. From this point on the film relies heavily on visuals rather than dialogue and in doing so manages brilliantly to convey both menace and the dazzling clockwork intricacy of Myra's plan to exterminate her betrayers.

These lines from the review of the film by "Kate Cameron" (*nom de plume* of women film critics at the *New York Daily News* for nearly half a century) capture the laudatory critical consensus nicely: "'Sudden Fear' is the sort of thriller that Hollywood made famous and then abandoned for more serious but duller films that carried messages of one sort or another. It is high time that some producer other than Alfred Hitchcock took it upon himself to bring suspense and excitement back to the screen with a capital S and a capital E." In my view *Sudden Fear* merited an Academy Award nomination for best picture as well as for best adapted screenplay (Myra's line to Les, delivered by Crawford with delicious irony, *"I was just wondering what I'd done to deserve you,"* is *All About Eve* level genius), best score and best film editing, but in the event Crawford and Kaufman had to settle for acting nominations for Crawford and Palance (for supporting actor), along with a richly merited nomination for Charles Lang for best black and white cinematography and Sheila O'Brien for costume design. (Crawford's costumes, hair and makeup get no fewer than six mentions in the credits.)

Gloria Grahame, who was dressed off the track, missed a nomination for the film, although she was nominated—and won—for her striking performance in *The Bad and the Beautiful*. Had she not received the nod for the latter flick, opines Robert Lentz, Grahame "almost certainly would have been nominated for *Sudden Fear*." This would be the last of Crawford's three best actress nominations and the first of Palance's three supporting actor nods. (After losing the next year for *Shane*, he would win an Oscar nearly forty years later for the comedy *City Slickers*, memorably interrupting his acceptance speech to do some one-armed push-ups.)

In the film there are essentially, aside from the principal trio, just two significant characters. Myra's attorney Steve Kearney, who in actuality more resembles another character from the book, Miles Street, is played by Bruce Bennett. Bennett, who had played the recessive husband of Joan Crawford's title character in *Mildred Pierce*, beat out Richard Egan, who had played Joan Crawford's recessive husband in *The Damned Don't Cry*, for the part. Steve Kearney's younger brother, "Junior" Kearney, played by future *Mannix* star Mike Connors in his first film role, has no existence whatsoever in the book, but in the film he takes on Steve's function as Irma's smitten dupe. Another important character from the book, Dr. Van Roan (Van Roon in the book), is reduced to a walk-on part of a line or two, while Myra's secretary Eve Taylor (Ann in the film) fares little better. Lily, Myra's sympathetically-presented black maid, who in the novel's proceedings plays a small but pivotal ironic role, does not feature at all in the film. Overall, the book is richer and more complex (Myra is far less likeable but more interesting, while there are suggestions from the author that Irma is a sociopathic lesbian), yet the film remains a wonderful cinematic achievement. When a restored version of the film was released by the Cohen Media Group in 2016, critics—this time a new generation of internet critics—once again gave *Sudden Fear* an enthusiastic round of applause.

What Edna Sherry made of all the fuss over her book and its film adaptation is unknown. Edna seems to have strenuously avoided publicity after her son Ernie's very public and highly embarrassing collision in 1930 with a pair of designing young sisters by the names of Nedra and Audrey, to the extent that I have never read an interview with her or even seen her picture in the papers or on the backs of book jackets. But although she was a Jew from Cincinnati by birth, the daughter of a man who made his pile in the retail clothing trade, she clearly came to know her way around New York society. Her husband, dentist Ernest Sherry, was a brother of the fabulously wealthy Louis Sherry, a once-famed restauranteur, hotelier, caterer and confectioner, whose luxury chocolates still are sold today, in colorfully decorated containers. In *Sudden Fear* Edna makes nods to her late, celebrated brother-in-law when she mentions a Sherry chocolate box a couple of times and gives Myra a beach "cottage" in Manhasset, which Louis back in the Twenties had purchased, a fabulous chateaux style mansion that he dubbed "Sherryland." Probably Edna took her sudden fame with aplomb. After all, she had had ample time in her life to learn that creative writing was altogether a hit-and-miss affair, and that even the best-laid plans for achieving public fame—or vicious personal revenge—are apt to go awry.

—May 2023
Germantown, TN

Curtis Evans received a PhD in American history in 1998. He is the author of *Masters of the "Humdrum" Mystery: Cecil John Charles Street, Freeman Wills Crofts, Alfred Walter Stewart and British Detective Fiction, 1920-1961* (2012) and most recently the editor of the Edgar nominated *Murder in the Closet: Essays on Queer Clues in Crime Fiction Before Stonewall* (2017) and, with Douglas G. Greene, the Richard Webb and Hugh Wheeler short crime fiction collection, *The Cases of Lieutenant Timothy Trant* (2019). He blogs on vintage crime fiction at The Passing Tramp.

Sudden Fear
Edna Sherry

Author's Dedication—
TO MY MOTHER
With Thanks for Many Things

CHAPTER I

Gangsters take their victims for a ride, shoot them with an economy of effort and steel, deposit them in a lonely spot, and drive coolly away. Crooked trustees of estates and sinister family physicians—mentioned substantially in their victims' wills—hatch out ingenious plots and carry them to a fatal conclusion. Half-mad lovers—male and female—strike in the heat of passion and, if they control their hysteria after the event, sometimes get away with it. These gentry operate with smooth regularity between book covers.

But for the run-of-the-mill, upper-middle-class, law-abiding, convention-ridden public—in short, for you and me—murder is a tough chore. Psychologists maintain that at one time or another the best of us has murder in his heart. What holds us back? Why aren't there as many murders in the average household as on the average bookshelf?

So you're planning a murder? For love, hate, revenge, or money. Let's go.

Item: Shooting. Immensely effective but in your well-ordered existence in a metropolitan apartment with a maid in the kitchen, a family underfoot, and friends dropping in without warning, how procure a gun, how learn to shoot, how hide the thunderous blast of a shot? These silencers you read about—even if you could buy one, wouldn't it be immediately traced to you, to say nothing of the gun itself and the necessary license to possess it? You're still planning a murder. But it looks like a gun is out.

Item: Poison. Who of us has arsenic, strychnine, or atropine handy on the bathroom shelf? Vaguely you know that if you attempt to buy some, you've got to sign the druggist's book, which will damn you at the drop of an autopsy. Weed killer, the solid British stand-by; curare, the rare South American undetectable poison—how the devil will you come by either, in your daily round? Better give poison a miss.

Item: Strangling. Is your victim going to take it tamely, or will he get in a yell or two which will bring somebody running to catch you red-handed? Even with circumstances right and no outcry raised, how will you know when the stranglee is actually dead and won't revive to point the finger at you? After all, it is your first strangling. A risky method—for you or me.

Item: Stabbing. Quiet but messy. And how many of us have had that course in anatomy which insures the one effective stroke with instant death in its train? Suppose your knife glances off a rib or snaps in the middle? Where are you then? Isn't there something better than stabbing?

The good old blunt instrument, of course. That one we do have at hand, right in our living room. A book end, a poker, even that full bottle of Scotch. It looks as if we'd found the answer. One vigorous swing. Any amateur can fracture a skull. The most artless of us knows enough to wipe off our fingerprints. Well, that's settled.

Or is it? It is *our* living room, *our* blunt instrument. A hundred and seventy pounds of defunct humanity on our Saruk rug. Of course, if we can smuggle him out, we can breathe easy. Nothing, then, to connect us with him at all. But our apartment is 8 B. Elevator boy. Doorman. Tenants going in and out. What the hell do we do with him?

Murder is a tough chore.

CHAPTER II

Myra Hudson sat in the darkened orchestra, watching the rehearsal of her new play, *Immoral Courage*. With her smooth, shingled, graying hair, her arrogant, high-bred, clever-ugly face, she looked every day of her forty-two years. To the world, she was rather a formidable figure. All women and most men were afraid of her mordant wit and biting tongue. She had few friends, but she was one of the most sought-after women in America. There was good reason for this. She had practically everything except youth and beauty. The last in the long line of *the* Hudsons, she was important socially and financially. The Hudson "cottage" at Newport, the Palm Beach "hacienda" and the Rhinebeck "farm" had figured in the social columns as long as social columns had existed. She called half of *Who's Who* by their first names and snubbed nine-tenths of them as unutterable bores. To the solidity of the Hudson name and the Hudson fortune, Myra had added a very real luster by her own efforts. She had written seven plays in the last fifteen years, all of them brilliant and all of them successful. From coast to coast, a new "Myra Hudson" meant a tug of war among producers and a pitched battle in Hollywood to get there "fustest with the mostest." She was unmarried, lonely, and, except when hard at work, not very happy.

She watched the rehearsal with an inexplicable sense of dissatisfaction. The costars, Rhea Vine and Clay Harwood, were distilling the last fine drop of meaning from her sparkling lines. The rest of the cast of eight ranged from admirable to adequate. She could not put her finger on the cause of her dissatisfaction. But it was there. Harwood, in spite of his artistry, seemed a trifle shopworn. Rhea Vine's beauty had lost some of its freshness—one felt the masseuse and the beauty salon behind her perfection. They were delightful in their scenes together, but as soon as someone else entered the picture—as soon as this young—what was his name?—oh, Blaine— Suddenly Myra snapped her fingers. She had it!

Like a detective on the trail, she watched Lester Blaine enter for his small scene with Rhea. His part was a passive one. It required only striking good looks and enough charm to make him a convincing stalking horse in Rhea's attempt to win back an indifferent husband.

Blaine entered, crossed the stage, and paid his respectful homage to Rhea. He did it correctly, even well; he employed none of the sly tricks actors use to steal the limelight; but immediately, without effort, the center of interest shifted from Rhea to him. Suddenly nothing registered except this young, graceful, beautiful creature with the easy stride and the enchanting smile.

Myra examined him in detail. Six feet, at least, broad in the right places and flat in the right places; fine skin, tanned a good brown; sea-blue eyes and white teeth in flashing contrast;

features strong, regular but sensitively chiseled. Superlatively handsome—but Myra had seen thousands of handsome men in her day. This boy had something else—a grace, an aura of springtime, a nostalgic quality to materialize dreams. While he was on the stage, Rhea Vine dimmed to the unimportance of an understudy.

Myra turned to her secretary, Eve Taylor.

"Make a note for me to see Hixon about this Blaine."

Eve made the note, a little sorry for the boy. She recognized Myra's "thumbs down" tone. She wondered what Myra found wrong with him.

After a few moments, Myra asked her, "How does he strike you, Eve?" She had a good deal of respect for Eve's judgment, and where her work was concerned, she was always ready for intelligent criticism.

"Quite well. And gorgeous to look at."

"Overpowering. He takes all the shine out of Rhea. We'll have to get rid of him."

"That's a tough break. To lose a job because you're too handsome."

"A theatrical production isn't geared to good works. I can't have Rhea and Harwood overshadowed by this—male doll."

"He must have more than just looks if he can do that." Eve was young but she had perception.

She had first come to know Myra several years before, when Myra telephoned her secretarial agency for a pinch hitter while her own secretary was ill. For three weeks, Eve gave satisfaction in an unobtrusive, competent way. But the convalescent secretary, taking another week at Atlantic City for recuperation, suddenly met her future on the boardwalk, spun through a whirlwind courtship, and resigned as Myra's secretary to assume the joys of married bliss.

Myra, annoyed and disorganized by this defection, considered the matter and finally spoke to Eve.

"Miss Taylor, I would like a short autobiographical sketch of your life."

Eve stared.

"Parents, background, prospects, ambitions. The truth,

please."

"I live with my parents in Englewood, New Jersey. My father's a retired major in the United States Army. He has what they call a 'heart condition,' and they're living on his pension. That was the end of Vassar for me, and I took up secretarial work. I don't think my ambitions are any of your affair."

"They are very much my affair. My present secretary has had the bad judgment to marry and leave me flat. I am considering you for the post. You are young, pretty, with a certain amount of charm. If this is a stopgap between girlhood and matrimony, I won't consider you. I can't have my work disrupted by avoidable externals."

"I have no immediate intentions—or prospects—of getting married." Eve's lips twitched, and her dark-fringed gray eyes danced.

"You relish the vista of secretaryship for life?"

"Oh, no."

"What *is* in your mind?"

"You won't like it, Miss Hudson."

"Then I'd best know it now."

"I hope, someday, to write, myself."

"You feel yourself qualified?"

"Not yet. I'm just twenty-one."

"You speak with the wisdom of the ages."

"I know enough to know I know nothing."

Myra laughed appreciatively.

"That has a real ring to it. It's very nearly an epigram. I should want you to live here with me. What would your people say?"

"They'd think it the chance of a lifetime for me to see how Myra Hudson works."

"You'll earn whatever you glean. I'm a slave driver. Intolerant, impatient. I expect perfection."

"You won't get it but you'll get the best that's in me."

"That will have to do, I suppose. The pay is extremely good. Outside working hours, you will consider yourself a member of my household, free to come and go as you please and welcome socially when I have guests. Shall we consider it settled?"

Eve hesitated, and Myra raised her eyebrows somewhat ominously.

"Well, Miss Taylor?"

Eve looked distressed.

"I'm waiting," said Myra.

"I can't help it!" Eve burst out. "I'd give my right eye for the job but I've got to tell you, even if you're furious. I've watched this play you're doing develop, and you're all wrong about the character of Victoria. No girl worth her salt would do what you've made her do." She stopped, appalled at her own nerve.

Myra gave her a steady appraising look.

"Sit down," she said quietly. "What *would* Victoria have done?"

In the years that followed, the relationship between Myra and Eve had deepened into a strong bond. Myra was often arrogant and intolerant, as she had promised, but just as often she took pains to explain to Eve how and why she developed a scene as she did, or when a gesture was worth more than five lines of dialogue.

Eve's feeling for Myra was mixed. She worshiped her creative ability and conceded her the right to a certain amount of temperament. But she sensed a ruthlessness and an essential egotism in Myra which chilled her. She never confided in her because she felt that Myra's interest in her personal affairs was nil—unless she could use them as material. They got along well on the surface. Myra was a gracious hostess to the girl. She made unexpected gestures of generosity, such as entering her as a guest member at Green Hollow, so that Eve could keep up her tennis; and presenting her with a handsome little Ford convertible one Christmas. The Ford, standing beside Myra's Chrysler in the garage behind the Sutton Place house was a constant reproach to Eve for the coolness of her personal feelings toward Myra. But she could never get beyond her original attitude. To her, Myra's talent was something to admire, but Myra's intolerance and self-absorption were repellent.

Eve would have been surprised if she had known how vulnerable Myra really was—in one respect. In spite of her keen mind and sharp wit, Myra was a slave to her love of youth and beauty. Time and again, she had interested herself in some young girl or man, giving them the aid of her influence and purse. It was notable that they were always good to look at. She surrounded herself with attractive people, often mistakenly attributing ability to them where beauty was their only asset. Although she would have burned with anger at the idea, this subconscious yearning rendered her defenseless and slightly pathetic.

CHAPTER III

Four weeks later, *Immoral Courage* opened with wild acclaim in New York. Lester Blaine was not in the cast.

Instead, he sat alone in the last row of the second balcony, and it was clear that he paid less attention to the stage than to the standees behind him. The second act curtain brought a storm of electric enthusiasm. People were on their feet, shouting with full throats as they beat their hands in a thunder of applause. Lester, timing his move, made his way to the cross aisle back of the balcony and approached a woman dressed in inconspicuous street clothes.

"I think you need a drink, Miss Hudson," he said, coming up behind her.

Myra frowned. It annoyed her to be recognized. Even after seven successful openings, first nights were an ordeal to her, and she still shunned friends and publicity, watching the premiere from the anonymity of the second balcony. Most people knew this idiosyncrasy of hers.

"If I do," she said coldly, "I am well able to get it for myself."

'That's your trouble. You're too darn able for your own good."

Myra turned to quell this impertinence with a word. She recognized him immediately—his was not an easy face to forget—and the word died on her lips. He stood looking down at her, a half-smile in his eyes. She stood, just looking at him. Again she felt the glamour she had sensed at rehearsal, which had eclipsed the stars of her play. To her own surprise, the cutting remark was not forthcoming.

The smile in Lester's eyes vanished. With a sort of unstudied dignity, he said, "Look, Miss Hudson. You did me a very dirty trick. I could be down there taking calls with the company. I could be sitting pretty with a two-year run on my hands. Hixon was satisfied with my work. But you went over his head and fired me. Why, I don't know. I think you owe me an explanation."

"I think I do," she replied quietly. She told herself she was only being just. The truth was, she wanted to go on looking at him. "I'll take that drink if it's still going." Her casual acceptance was the start of a race, a race between these two as to which of them could encompass the other's death first.

He took her arm and led her to one of the balcony exits, down an outside flight of iron stairs, and through the alley next to the theater, avoiding the crowds now pouring out into the lobby. He walked her nearly to Eighth Avenue before he steered her into a dim bar. They sat in one of the booths, and Blaine ordered Martinis. By this time, Myra's head was once more in charge.

She said satirically, "You know my first night coign of vantage; you know my favorite drink. Your scout work is A plus, Mr. Blaine."

He didn't smile.

"If you're interested enough, you get results," he said.

"I agree I do owe you an explanation for your dismissal—"

"Oh, that. Don't bother. I just used that as an excuse to get you out. You were trembling all through the second act. I thought if I could get your mind off yourself—"

"And why should you care if I was trembling?"

"You got me." He did smile now, his blue eyes crinkling joyously, his white teeth flashing. "I've been asking myself for a month why I keep thinking of you. But I don't stop."

"Perhaps your resentment keeps me in mind."

"What resentment?"

"I did get you fired, and you knew it."

"That's all in the game—it's happened before. I figure Harwood put the bee on you. He's pushing forty-five, and I've got this Greek puss as a handicap."

To her great surprise, Myra laughed.

"I should think your 'Greek puss' would be an asset."

"It's a damned nuisance. The other GIs ribbed me all over

Burma and India. Before that, it got in my way every time I got a call. I wasn't good enough for leads, and my face was usually too fancy for our hero to buck."

"Maybe you'd better take up riveting," Myra chuckled.

"Too many babes."

"You don't like—babes?"

"Not much. That's why I don't get this angle about you."

"I'm hardly a—babe."

"Could be. I mean you're past the gush stage. You're smooth, you know your way around, a guy can *talk* to you."

"How old are you, Mr. Blaine?"

"Twenty-seven."

"I'm fifteen years older."

"Well, swell! That evens things up some. I'm young and easy to look at. You're rich and famous. Each got something to offer. We ought to be friends."

Myra drew back into herself.

"You also have speed to offer, it seems. You're going a little too fast for my taste."

Lester smiled, undisturbed.

"Well, anyway, I've kept you from the jitters for the last ten minutes. That was the whole idea." He looked at his wristwatch. "If you want to catch the third act, we'd better be moving."

Myra sat still, staring at him. "You mean to tell me you brought me here solely to save me from first night nerves?"

He met her eyes steadily. "Look," he said softly. "Get it through your head. Whatever happens to you is important to me. It's crazy. But it's true."

The third act of *Immoral Courage* was performed without the presence of its author and its ex-juvenile. Over more Martinis, Myra and Lester sat talking in an easy, relaxed truce.

She even asked questions and heard the usual drab details of life in a small town, unrelieved by color, money, or opportunity. In Lester Blaine's case, opportunity had finally come when he was eighteen. That summer, when he was doing as little work as he dared and still keep his job as garageman, his *dea ex machina* appeared from her Lincoln limousine. The Lincoln limped in with a cracked cylinder head. Parts had to be sent for. The lady, annoyed at the delay and completely at a loose end, relieved her boredom by concentrating on the most attractive feature of the landscape. This was Lester. She felt it was a waste for such beauty to be hidden under a bushel. Being sixty, rich, and a patroness of the arts, she offered to finance him in a year's study in dramatics in New York. Lester, burning for any change at all, would have agreed to study paleontology, if such had been the lady's wish. Having no ties or affairs to delay him, when the Lincoln was ready, he was ready, too.

He found that he liked theatrical life and did not do too badly at it. He was already getting small parts when, in 1942, misfortune overtook him. His benefactress died suddenly without remembering Lester in her will. Added to that, a month later the draft got him.

Except for the hard work, he liked army life, with its companionship and complete lack of responsibility. The few scrimmages that he was in were offset by the fact that he was fed, housed, and clothed by a benevolent government. After his separation, he had landed two parts, but both plays had folded early. The role in *Immoral Courage* would have really put him on the map, but he still had a good part of his army pay to fall back on, and something would turn up. He was cheerful, optimistic, and entirely unresentful.

Around midnight, they had scrambled eggs and waited for the morning papers. Together, they read the unanimous accolades. With one voice, the press hailed the play, prophesying a longer run for it than *Life With Father* or *State of the Union*. Lester's genuine delight in her success touched Myra. There was something so decent, so boyish and wholehearted in his attitude, that she wanted to make it up to him. She ran over in her mind what producers and authors were casting at the moment. A word from her would help him immeasurably. But she said nothing. Instead, irrationally, she invited him to dine at her house, two nights later.

CHAPTER IV

The dinner was informal. Myra and Eve were the only women. Besides Lester, there were the three men Myra knew best in the world. One of them, Edgar Van Roon, a soft-spoken, idealistic man, had been in love with her since childhood. They had learned to swim together at Bailey's Beach; they had suffered together at dancing school and had later abjured the fashionable world for hard work. Van Roon was now a well-known physician. Myra had a sort of affection for him, but she had lorded it over him for too many years to consider him as a husband. It was inevitable that a self-effacing man like Van Roon should adore an autocratic woman like Myra. He accepted the mild role of friend with characteristic resignation.

There was Miles Street, the junior member of Street, Wyatt, and Street, who handled Myra's enormous inherited fortune honestly and cleverly. He was thirty-five, levelheaded, realistic, with a pleasing, ugly face and a quizzical sense of humor. He appreciated Myra's almost masculine brain but had no illusions as to her character. It was only of late that he had begun to appear regularly at the Sutton Place house in a social way. He admitted somewhat ruefully to himself that this was because Eve Taylor's wide-set gray eyes and shining black hair had begun to disturb his peace of mind.

Finally, there was Steve Thatcher, the only one of the three not of Myra's social class. Steve was a brilliant criminal lawyer whose entry into a case was practically synonymous with acquittal; whose capacity for liquor was only exceeded by his thirst. He had a mobile, impish face, a thatch of red hair, and a smile to melt juries. Myra had met him ten years before, when they had both spoken at an anti-Nazi rally at Carnegie Hall. His breezy personality, his fruity slang, and his undoubted brains attracted her. Steve always swore that her only attraction was that she had the best Scotch in New York. As a matter of fact, he often came to her with a tough psychological problem arising from his legal work and seldom left without having clarified it by discussion with her. He received fabulous retainers and spent just as fabulously. But the red thatch hid a level head. He made many shrewd investments, tipped off by insiders, and owned several valuable parcels of Manhattan real estate. The latest of these was a huge apartment house on Fifty-Seventh Street, a block away from Myra's home, where he lived in a bachelor's Eden in the nineteen-room penthouse.

Eve, in a dark red crepe, looked delightful, her irregular features unaccountably adding up to charm if not beauty. Myra, in severe, expertly cut Schiaparelli black, looked distinguished but undeniably plain.

With only six at table, the talk was general. Steve, after a good many highballs, revealed indiscreetly the truth behind a current murder trial in which his client, a well-known New York playboy, had come off with flying colors.

"Any ambulance chaser could have got him off," he finished. "All the real evidence had to be kept out. Otherwise, two senators and a billionaire dollar-a-year man would have had to resign. You see, *they* knew the lady as intimately as my client did. The judge made it very clear in his summing up, how he expected the jury to find."

"And you call that justice!" Eve said with a snort.

"The gal was dead, anyway," said Lester. "Why ruin important people?" It was his first remark. All three men turned their eyes on him. Van Roon, in his gentle way, was shocked. Steve, freshening his drink to a deep amber, decided the kid was more than a mere valentine. Miles, his eyes shuttling from Lester to Eve to Myra, frowned and wondered what Lester was doing there at all. If he was Eve's friend, it was bad, he thought glumly, and if Myra's, not much better. As custodian of the twelve-million-dollar Hudson estate, he had had a few scares over fortune hunters. Myra was so damned unconventional in her choice of friends. However, she was levelheaded and usually knew the score. Still, it would be a load off his mind if she'd do the sensible thing and marry the trustworthy Edgar Van Roon.

The talk veered to Myra's play and opening night.

"What happened to you?" Steve asked indignantly. "I give the biggest damn party of the year and my guest of honor never shows up! I'm claiming a foul."

"I forgot where you live, Steve," Myra said solemnly.

"No soap. Why didn't you come?"

"If you claim a foul, I'll claim temperament. I just couldn't face a crowd that night."

"That's a lot of hooey. Nobody likes a big hand better than you. Where were you?"

"If you must know, I was committing a murder," she retorted demurely.

"That's different. Give me a ring when you need me."

Through all this, Lester never batted an eyelash. Myra noticed that there was no wise, in-the-know gleam in his blue eyes, no sophisticated smirk on his well-cut lips. She had been with him from ten until half past two on opening night, she had passed up a smart, important party, and she was keeping it a secret. He took it in his stride. Such discretion piqued her interest. As she said good night to him, she asked him to a cocktail party for the following week.

She asked him to several parties. She began to be seen with him in public. She introduced him to more of her friends. The only thing she did not do was to help him toward a part in any play.

There was, of course, a good deal of talk. Anything that Myra Hudson did was news, but this came under the category of headlines. Miles Street and Eve Taylor wasted half of a perfectly good evening that should have been devoted solely to themselves, in discussing it.

"It's calamitous, that's what it is!" he railed. "This pretty little lap dog, this blue-eyed fortune hunter—"

"Oh, Miles, stop it. He's not bad at all, really. He's good-natured—"

"Why wouldn't he be? Sunning himself in the Hudson name—"

"You're nothing but a snob, Miles Street! I wonder you talk to *me*. My people are just plain army, and we never saw hair nor hide of the *Mayflower*."

"Oh. *You*. You've got brains and breeding and innate loveliness. What's this gigolo got but his looks?"

"Thanks for the plug. If Myra likes him—"

"How can she, for God's sake?"

"Well, she seems to."

"You really think she's serious?"

"Yes, I do. And if you must know, I think he's good for her. She's not nearly as autocratic and snooty as she was. She's softer, somehow."

"Oh, Lord!" He groaned. "This is it. It's positively tragic."

"But why? Suppose she is older than he is. She's got so much else to offer—her brains, her ability—"

"Just the things *he* wouldn't appreciate. He'll let her down. And then there'll be hell to pay."

"Don't be such an alarmist."

"You don't know Myra. She's got her good points, so long as she isn't crossed. But let anybody tweak that oversized vanity of hers, and she shows all the gentle traits of a jaguar. I've known her to ruin a woman socially because she said Myra looked like a purse-proud walnut. Even as a kid, she had to be cock of the walk or else."

"They tell tales about every famous person."

"Well, here's one about her. I grant it's only rumor, but a good many people believe it. A few years ago, she took up a good-looking politician who was beginning to make a name for himself. He was strictly on the make and had ideas about using Myra. He got hold of some inside information that the government was going to buy up a certain tract of ground for a naval airport. The land was worthless, just sand dunes, actually. He asked Myra to lend him the money to buy it in, planning to stick the government by asking a whopping price for it. Of course, it would all have to be done through dummies, and his name couldn't appear at all. Myra's got sound views about her country and refused. That same night at his club, somebody twitted this chap about Myra. He'd had a few drinks too many and he was slightly less than discreet in his reply. He said she was all right as a step up the ladder, but he couldn't sit across from that face at breakfast, not even if it meant the White House."

"Well, if she was furious, I don't blame her."

"Nor I. But Myra wasn't merely furious. She took steps."

"What could she do?"

"I don't know the details. I only know two facts for certain. My father was managing Myra's estate at the time and he says that she came and demanded two million dollars cash without explanation."

"I don't quite—"

"The other fact is that when the government came to locate the owners of the tract, in order to buy, they discovered that every acre was in the possession of one man, the deeds were all on record in his name, and that every foot of ground had been bought within the last month. Of course, the man was this politician. There was a very dirty scandal, the chap came close to going to jail, and of course was utterly done for politically."

"You mean she deliberately threw away two million dollars, so that he'd look guilty of using government information?"

"It was rather subtle, at that. Actually, he was crooked enough to *want* to cheat the government and was innocent only because he hadn't the money to swing it. Myra swung it for him. His clever deal became a deadly boomerang. And of course he was booted out of the club where he had been so outspoken about Myra's looks."

"It's hard to believe she'd go to such lengths."

"Well, my dear Eve, you're not obliged to believe it. I've told it to you for what it's worth to show you what could happen if Myra tangles with some worthless adventurer who lets her down."

"Why should you assume Lester Blaine is an adventurer and that he *will* let her down? I think perhaps she's got something he feels a need for—a sort of half-maternal—I can't quite put it in words. Perhaps he *would* like a life of ease, that her money *is* part of her attraction. But I think he may really care for her, too. I *do* know he doesn't look twice at girls. He doesn't know *I'm* on earth, for instance."

"Then he's an even duller fool than I thought." Miles grinned. "And if you ask me, I'm a bit fed up for the moment with Myra. Did anyone ever tell you that you have a very intriguing little nose?"

CHAPTER V

Myra's play, settling down for its long run, left her somewhat at loose ends. She took a short breathing spell before attacking new work. A good deal of this time she spent with Lester. She took him often to lunch at the Colony Club, where he got a tremendous kick out of the fact that the people who stopped to greet Myra all bore names which were bywords in the society columns.

His manner toward Myra was a nice mixture of admiration, affection, and deference, without ever becoming servile. He made no bones about his financial position, and when he settled the check, it was for a modest meal in either a Chinese or an Italian restaurant. Their talk was, perforce, entirely personal. He did not attempt to measure up to her intellectually. He noticed everything she wore and commented on it. If her hair was brushed back a little flatter than usual, he would say, "I love that sleek look you've got about you tonight. It gives you a sort of classic effect." If she wore a yellow blouse under her suit, he would say, "Yellow's perfect for you. It brings out all the gold tints in your skin."

When one is inclined to be sallow, it is pleasant to have it designated as gold. Still, Myra was no fool. Her mind and her mirror told her the truth, but he was so spontaneous about it, that he half convinced her. And he never overdid it. There was always a saving grace of lightness which kept it from cloying.

"Look, baby, so you're not the Queen of Sheba or Miss Atlantic City. See if I care. I'm so fed up on good looks, mine and everybody else's, that I'd pick your odd little face with its character and distinction out of any beauty show. The hell with long eyelashes. For me, you've got what it takes."

She finally believed him—because she wanted to; because his looks, his grace, his enchanting smile and glamorous aura appealed to her so poignantly. For the first time in her life, the impregnable, self-sufficient, strong-minded Myra was at the mercy of her feelings.

They were lunching at the Colony Club on the day that the papers carried rumors of a colossal offer for the picture rights to *Immoral Courage*. The occasion gave Lester his chance.

"This is a stickup," he said, leaning toward her.

"I'm reaching." She smiled back. "What have I got that's so valuable?"

"Don't start me, honey. Everything about you is that." He dropped his light tone as he went on. "Jokes aside, Myra, would you do something for me?"

"Of course. What is it?"

"You told me why I lost the part in your play. The reason doesn't hold for the Hollywood version. I wouldn't take the shine out of any screen stars. A line from you would cinch the part for me. Would you write the line?"

From under his lashes, he watched her, holding his breath. For a few moments she was silent. The silence was so eloquent to Lester that he let out his breath in a sigh of relief. She didn't want him to go. The rest would be easy.

"You—think you'd like Hollywood?" she asked at last.

"I'm getting nowhere here. I haven't really much to offer but my appearance. And that pays off better on the Coast."

"Hollywood's a mad sort of place. You'd hate it," she said.

"I'll take a chance," he said firmly. The more she objected, the surer he was of her.

There was a long pause. He leaned back and waited. She sat, eyes lowered, scraping her cigarette-end against the side of the ash tray. Finally, she looked up and met his eyes.

"Don't go, Lester," she said in a low tone.

"I really need it, Myra," he said quietly. In a minute, she'd drop into his hands like a ripe plum.

There was another pause before she said slowly, "You don't— need it, Lester. Anything you want—"

"No, thanks, dear. Money isn't going to spoil *our* friendship."

"Money isn't as important as you think, Les."

"Not if you've got it."

"That's true. I've heaps of it, too much for one person. Why not let me share it?"

"Money's the one thing that can only be shared if you're

married."

"Are you going to make me ask you, Les?" she said, with an effort. He leaned forward impulsively, his whole face alight.

"Darling! This isn't happening! You mean you—you—the great Myra Hudson—I never would have *dared*—I'm dreaming—"

"You're not dreaming, Les."

He closed his hand hard over hers.

"Darling! Darling! Can I say all I've had bottled up in me ever since I first saw you? If I say I love you, you swear you won't vanish?"

"Try it, Les. I'll be here," she said with a shaky laugh.

They were married a week later.

The columnists had a field day with not-too-friendly cracks about the ham who knew on which side his bread was buttered. Myra's circles, both socialite and professional, were genuinely shocked. Unanimously, they predicted disaster.

They were all wrong. The marriage was a success. Myra and Lester were thoroughly happy. He put his whole soul into his efforts to please her. When they were alone, he never forgot to use some form of endearment when he spoke to her. He thought up a dozen little surprises a day and seemed to enjoy them as much as she did. He was always ready to run her most trivial errands, often changing his own plans with the sunniest good humor.

The wellspring of this devotion was, of course, pure gratitude. He adored her for the silken sheets on his bed, the endless smooth service which he could summon by a mere ring for a servant, above all, for the custom-built Cadillac convertible which was his alone. To his immature, luxury-starved nature, every day was Christmas—and Myra was Santa Claus. In his uncomplex soul, there was only delight—certainly no embarrassment—in the fact that she put a monthly check for spending money into his bank account and paid the bills for his elaborate wardrobe.

For her part, Myra was experiencing a totally new sensation. She was being made much of, not for her brains or her importance, but as something small, fragile, and feminine.

Under the treatment, she softened surprisingly. If she played Lady Bountiful, she was gracious and tactful, about it. But it is difficult to change the habits of forty-two years. There were still occasional flashes of autocracy and arrogance, along with her affection and indulgence for Lester.

She still kept up with her old world of mental values. Lester realized his limitations and made no attempt to swim in deep waters. He showed no trace of jealousy of the intellectual sessions she held with Edgar, Miles, and Steve—her "brain trust," Lester called them. That was over his head, and he was the first to admit it. They could have her brains, he was fond of saying, if he could have her heart.

He caused practically no change in the smooth routine of the household. He merely moved in, was assigned his own suite of rooms and was careful not to be underfoot while the important business of Myra's day was in progress.

From nine until one, she did her prescribed stint of creative work into her Dictaphone, while Eve transcribed yesterday's output in another room. Later, unless Myra wanted him to accompany her to the country club, he went about his own absorbing but innocuous amusements, while Myra's masseuse, hairdresser, and dressmaker contrived to keep her fit and reasonably young-looking. He always reported on the dot for escort duty when she was ready to relax.

Life was a continuous delight to him. Like all adolescents, he was a game player. He threw himself into the learning of golf with real zest and actually became excellent at it. Tennis he found too strenuous for his essential indolence, but he got a supreme thrill out of zooming along at ninety miles in the Cadillac. At Myra's suggestion, he took bridge lessons, and while he learned to hold his own without disgrace, he never really understood the game. He made a cult of mixing drinks and gained a certain vogue among Myra's set for his skill in that line. He was always polite to the servants—and popular—but he never tired of querying Austin, Myra's butler, when drinks were in progress, as to whether the glasses were chilled, whether Austin had remembered the lemon-zest, or if the nutmeg was freshly ground. If Myra thought these petty enthusiasms childish and immature, one look at his eager face took the edge from her impatience and substituted an amused indulgence.

He got along well with Eve. He respected her, was polite and friendly, but she could have been eighty for all the personal interest he took in her. And Eve liked him. His frank enjoyment of luxury, his naïve wonder at his own luck, and his complete devotion to Myra were all endearing.

When the serious business of the day was over, Myra and Lester sallied forth to cocktail parties, dinners, theater, or bridge together. He was always a credit to her. His looks and charm hid his lack of intellect, especially as he had the sense to keep his mouth shut when the discussions were over his head. When Myra entertained in her own home, he proved to be an excellent host.

It was, of course, inevitable that so handsome a creature should have a certain vogue of his own. Several of Myra's young friends—and some not so young—rushed him with varying degrees of brazenness. He passed through their fire totally unsinged. He was courteous, friendly, gay but never intimate. Either he was peculiarly indifferent to the feminine in all its forms or else he was still too enamored of the costly toys and luxuries which were heaped on him, to have time or inclination for dalliance. So far, he was true to Myra, mentally and physically.

Little by little, Myra's friends began to drop their disparaging tone and even succumbed to his unfailing good nature. After a year, a good many liked him for his own sake, making due allowances for his limitations.

Myra's three intimates had distinctly varying views. Miles Street, as custodian of Myra's huge fortune, was unflaggingly suspicious. Below Lester's ingenuous surface, he was constantly searching for the fortune hunter. He nearly went on his knees—to no avail—to prevent Myra from making a will in his favor.

Edgar Van Roon, who presumably should have hated a successful rival, accepted Lester wholeheartedly. Steve Thatcher had a sneaking respect for this nobody who had pulled himself up by his own bootstraps, but resented that a woman of Myra's brains and achievements should swallow his guff merely because it issued from a handsome mouth. While he and Myra wrangled unceasingly, she had a special niche in his irreverent heart. Mentally he promised that if this young cub sold her out, he would knock his block off.

CHAPTER VI

Immoral Courage, had been running to capacity for more than a year on Broadway. Myra had finally sold the picture rights at a stupendous sum. But it was not in her to rest on her laurels. She had the real writer's temperament and could no more stop weaving new situations and dialogue than she could stop breathing. Her interest in *Immoral Courage* was nil; she was completely wrapped up in the problems of a new play. She worked hard and competently but she had struck a snag. For four mornings, she had dictated steadily into the patient Dictaphone, and four times, on hearing the machine play back her product, she had discarded the cylinders and started again at scratch. But the play wasn't marching.

Finally she realized that she was mentally tired. At dinner that night—they happened to be alone—she said to Lester, "Tell Austin to pack a bag for you. We're going down to the Hut tomorrow."

Lester, far from resenting something very like an order, responded with enthusiasm. "Swell! Don't bring Eve along, and we'll have a new little honeymoon."

"You're nice," she said patting his hand.

"You bet I'm nice," he grinned. "I always am when I get what I want."

"Take a bathing suit. If this weather keeps up, the bathing will be wonderful."

"For a water rat like you, maybe," he said with a wry face. "For me, swimming's never a bargain. And in early June, it's just plain punishment."

"You'll see. The Cove's so protected, you don't get any wind. I've often gone in much earlier than this."

"You swim, and I'll watch. The water takes the curl out of my eyelashes."

"You're just bone-lazy, you—you landlubber."

"Can I help it if I was brought up inland without even a 'crick' within miles?"

"I suppose I'll have to teach you to fish, too."

"I don't want to learn. All I want is to have you to myself without you tearing yourself to bits over a second act tag line."

"So you're jealous of my work?"

"I'm jealous of every minute in the day when I'm not monopolizing you hook, line, and sinker."

He kissed her hand, which still lay over his. Austin, the august butler, entering to remove the bouillon cups, suppressed a snort at what he called—to Mrs. Link, the cook—their bloody billing and cooing.

The Hut was a comfortable eight-room cottage on the Sound, its extensive grounds sloping right down to the horseshoe beach. Myra had bought it years ago with some of the first important money she had earned. She liked it better than any of her more pretentious estates. Mr. and Mrs. Foster lived there all year round as caretakers, and cooked and served competently whenever Myra came down for a breathing spell.

The weather held. It was more like midsummer than the beginning of June. Peonies were in full bloom, and early roses perfumed the soft breeze. The tender, incredible green of the budding trees shed an exquisite light.

They spent the whole first day on the beach, Myra's tense, muscular little body soaking in sun and air. She slept twelve solid hours that night.

On the second morning, as they loafed on the beach, she announced her intention of taking a swim. But when Lester urged her to go in while he sunned himself on the sand, she lingered. And when he shifted his head onto her lap, she put off her swim contentedly.

"Tell me, honey. Are you sick of your bargain? Do you wish you'd never laid eyes on me?" he asked, after a while.

Myra ran her fingers through his thick yellow mop.

"It was one of the smartest things my eyes ever did," she said lightly. But she could hardly keep the tremor out of her voice. She did her utmost not to go maudlin over him, but he was so boyish, so handsome, and so engaging, that her heart went out to him. She would have loved to tell him unreservedly how much he meant to her, but her innate pride and her sense of fitness kept her silent. Instead, she pushed him unceremoniously off her lap, pulled on her bathing cap, and said, "You can't blarney me out of my swim, you loafer. I need exercise."

"Oh. So it's exercise you want. Okay. I'll race you up the beach. And the last one there is a rotten egg!" He tore off over the smooth sand, his superb body flashing in the sun. Myra sprinted after him but was no match for his long legs. At the east point of the cove, he stopped and caught her up in his arms.

"That'll learn you, shorty. Can you stagger back or must I tote you?" From the vantage point of his shoulder, she kicked her heels against his hard stomach.

"Let me down, you big bully."

"Am I a loafer? Am I? Am I?" His free hand explored her ribs. She squirmed and squealed.

"Stop it! I'm ticklish! Let me down!"

"Am I a—"

"Les! Quick! Look out there!" The urgency of her tone stopped him.

"Where? What is it?"

"Beyond the point—something—somebody—"

He looked where she pointed, far out on the crisp ruffled blue water.

"Yeah—something shiny. Like the knob on a brass bed," he said, unexcited.

"It's a head—a person!" She scrambled down his body like a squirrel and was tearing to the water's edge before he realized her intention. By the time he did, and yelled to her, she was well out in the water, swimming with smooth, steady strokes toward the "knob on a brass bed." It was a long swim, and twice the knob disappeared from his view as he watched breathlessly. But it bobbed up again, and he noticed that Myra's course never swerved from a straight line toward it.

After minutes of paralysis, Lester dashed up the slope to where Foster was pruning the hedge.

"Foster! Quick! Get out the *Flicker!* Miss Myra—" His gesture told as much as his words. Foster dropped his shears and ran toward the boathouse. Luckily, when Myra had phoned of her approaching visit, Foster had made the speedboat shipshape. In five minutes, they were skimming like a sea bird in Myra's wake. The knob was now unquestionably a human head, its water-sleek yellow hair gleaming in the sun. As Foster slowed to turn and approached it, Myra reached it. Arms appeared, flailing and clutching at her, dragging her under. She bobbed up and with a neat, expert precision, struck the edge of her hand against the neck below the yellow hair. The arms dropped nervelessly. Myra, grasping a solid handful of the yellow hair, turned shoreward.

"Myra! Over here!" Lester shouted.

Myra's little bright eyes flashed in their direction. She grinned and made for the boat, never loosing her grip on the yellow hair.

CHAPTER VII

Hours later, Myra awoke in her twin bed. She felt wonderful but ravenously hungry. As she sat up, the other twin bed came into view. It was occupied by a complete stranger. A naked girl was sitting up in the bed, combing her hair with the comb from Myra's dresser. The golden shimmer of the hair and the classic pose suggested a Lorelei, but apart from those aids, the girl could have qualified anywhere as a siren. Never, in Myra's extensive experience from Broadway to Hollywood, had she seen so beautiful a creature. The creamy magnolia skin was faintly flushed, not so much with color as with a sort of glow from within. The profile was pure and perfect, but saved from marble inanity by the rich human curve of the beautiful mouth. Myra caught the incredible length of the curling eyelashes against the sharp light from the window, and the equally breathtaking beauty of the forward-pushing small breasts.

Youth and beauty had a terrific pull for Myra. She stared,

spellbound, until the intensity of her gaze reached the girl in the bed. She turned and viewed Myra composedly.

"Hello," she said. "You're the one, aren't you? Who saved me, I mean. Thanks a lot." She went on combing her hair. Myra saw that her eyes were a cool pansy-blue.

"That's right. And were you a tough proposition! Tried to strangle me. I had to knock you out."

"So that's why my neck's sore."

"Sorry. If I hadn't clipped you, we'd have both gone under."

"Oh, you were right," said the girl dispassionately. "I've done it myself to people when I had to."

"How come a swimmer got stuck out there?"

"Cramp. My first swim of the year. Look. Are you as hungry as I am?"

Myra laughed. This blunt, beautiful girl delighted her.

"Starved. Mrs. Foster'll bring us up something." She rang the bell behind her bed. "You'll find a bed jacket in that closet. Bring me one, too, will you? Mrs. Foster doesn't hold with the nude in art."

The girl did as she was asked and wrapped herself in a handsome emerald-green housecoat. Then she brought a blue-and-white-striped terry-cloth robe to Myra, more utilitarian than beautiful. Myra concealed a grin. This girl knew what she wanted and went for it with an economy of effort.

Mrs. Foster, clucking over Myra like a hen over a duckling, brought them consommé, chicken salad, lemon pie, and coffee.

"You keep on taking swims like that at your age and you'll see where you land," she warned gloomily.

"Well, I couldn't very well stand and watch Miss—"

"Neves," said the girl.

"—Miss Neves drown, could I?"

"If she ain't young and strong enough to keep herself from drowning, let her stay on shore," pronounced Mrs. Foster uncompromisingly. It was plain that she considered the strange girl socially unworthy of the respect she tendered Myra and Myra's friends.

Myra changed the subject tactfully. Mrs. Foster's hedgehog propensities were offset by her superlative pies.

"Where's Mr. Blaine?"

"Still asleep. He was more trouble than the two of you. Near had high-sterics when you keeled over."

"*I* keeled over?" Myra echoed.

"Hit your head, getting in the boat, Foster says. The doctor give him a sleep powder."

"Well, don't disturb him. We'll take it easy a little longer."

"You want my advice, you'll stay in bed till tomorrow. I've dried out *her* bathing suit." She nodded her head toward the girl. "She can go as soon as she's ready."

"I'll let you know when to bring it up," said Miss Neves calmly.

Mrs. Foster shot her a look compounded of contempt and helpless fury and marched out of the room. They tackled the food without words.

The sharp edge of their appetite appeased, Myra said, "I'm Myra Blaine. You say your name's Neves?"

"Irma Neves."

"Floating population?"

"Oh, no. A native in poor standing. Couldn't you tell from Mrs. Foster's tone?"

"Mrs. Foster's a confirmed snob. You mustn't mind her."

"Don't worry, I don't, especially as she's got cause."

"You mean the 'poor standing' is deserved?"

"My father was the village drunk until a month ago."

"Oh? Reformed?"

"Dead."

"I'm sorry."

"You needn't be. The whole town was relieved. Me most of all."

"I can understand that. But why should they take it out on you?"

"I didn't show proper feeling when he died. Drunk or sober, he was my father. I should have cried and worn black. The night after his funeral, I went to the pictures."

"I see."

"They even went so far as to mutter that I helped his death along."

"How beastly! I admire your courage in living up to your convictions. Still—if you expect to live among these people—"

"I don't."

"You've made plans?"

"Yes."

"Don't be so stenographic."

"Seeing you saved it, I guess you're entitled to the story of my life."

"You mustn't mind my nosiness. It's just writer's itch."

"There's precious little in my life to interest a writer. My mother's been dead for years. My father was the local dentist. I've just sold what was left of his practice and equipment for a thousand dollars, and there's three hundred cash in the bank. I'm pulling out of this hole to found a future."

"Anything definite in view?"

"Certainly."

"Thirteen hundred isn't all the money in the world."

"Enough for my purpose."

"What is that purpose?"

"What would *you* do with my looks?"

Myra was conscious of disappointment. While Irma's beauty did warrant a stage or screen success, the girl's salty personality promised something fresher than a banal theatrical ambition.

"I suppose so," she said. "And I might be of help to you. I've got a few 'ins' in Hollywood."

"Hollywood! No, thanks."

"Oh? Must be the theater. What makes you think you can act?"

"Look. You've got me all wrong. I don't want any part of the stage."

"Well, what *was* your idea?"

"Nursing."

"Nursing!"

"You seem surprised."

"I really beg your pardon. I've been misjudging you. So you have a genuine call."

"Call, hell," replied Irma mildly. "You haven't been misjudging me."

"Well, I wish you'd put me right."

"It's this way, I'm out for certain things. Money, first and foremost."

"Aren't we all?" murmured Myra.

"Cars, clothes, service, travel. A place in the world. How do I get 'em?"

"Hardly in a hospital, I should think."

"I'm easy to look at. You have to give me that."

"Absolutely."

"Suppose I do go to Hollywood. The competition's terrific. They say every waitress in the town is stunning—all the Miss Whatevers who won contests but didn't get further than a screen test. Thirteen hundred'd be a drop in the bucket—clothes, swanky apartment, and so on. Why should I buck it?"

"You seem as wise as you are lovely."

"Whereas nursing—okay, I work like a dog till I'm a full-fledged R.N. It'll be worth it. Rich men get sick."

"I'm beginning to see the light."

"I study the field, take my time, and grab off what I'm looking for. There's no sucker like a convalescent capitalist."

Myra's mouth widened in a delighted grin. Her instinct had been right; Irma was a child of nature, uninhibited by any moral yardsticks. Her cool, unprincipled outlook gave her a fresh and candid originality which Myra's writing instinct itched to study and develop. She would hang onto the girl with just as conscienceless a determination as Irma's own. She would squeeze her dry and put the juice into a play.

"I can still be of help to you, I think," she said. "There are short cuts even in nursing. I'm a trustee of one of the swankiest hospitals in New York. You might as well start right, and it's no trouble to pull a wire or two."

"Swell. And ten to one, you know some Park Avenue doctors. Probably their patients would be rolling. That wouldn't hurt me, either."

At dinner, Myra watched curiously when she introduced Irma to Lester. Irma wore a black dinner dress of Myra's which fitted her slim, rounded body as well as it had fitted Myra's spare angular one, except that it cleared the floor by a couple of inches where it would have swept the ground on Myra. But one hardly noticed what Irma wore. One only saw her face and figure; her perfect features and thick rippling golden hair dominated her clothes as an exquisite rose will eclipse its vase.

Myra watched them together with a smug gusto. Her ego took credit for their looks. Others might surround themselves with charming men and pretty women, but she attracted the cream. Nothing less was Myra Hudson's due. She looked on them almost as creations of her own hand. It never occurred to her that if they had not been outwardly superlative she would never have given either a second thought. Lester's radiance covered a weak, greedy inanity, and Irma's, a cheap, cold calculation. But Myra's voracious love of beauty blinded her to their intrinsic worthlessness.

Lester greeted Irma civilly but was entirely concerned for Myra.

"You're *sure* you don't feel any effects of the bump?" he asked anxiously.

"I can't even find the place. Miles Street always says I'm hardheaded."

"Well, I guess it runs to a little celebrating." He mixed a shakerful of cocktails. Irma refused to drink without comment, but Myra guessed that her experience with her father had convinced her that alcohol could be no part of her program. She noticed, too, that the girl had no intention of being as frank with Lester as she had been with Myra. By a sort of gentleman's agreement, the two women kept Irma's cool philosophy a secret. All Lester heard was that Irma intended to take up nursing without delay.

At bedtime, Myra asked Lester, "What do you think of her?"

"Staggering. She's just wasted in a hospital. But I guess she's got the nursing temperament at that."

"What does that mean?"

"*You're* asking *me*, honey? As if you hadn't tagged her yourself."

"Tell me. I'm interested."

"She's as cold as a fish. You get close, and your teeth begin to chatter."

Myra regarded him with something like respect. "Y'know, dear, I've underestimated you."

"Is that bad?" He grinned.
"It's good. You've got perception."
"Over my head."
"Never mind. Did you like her?"
"Not much. Of course she's a treat to look at."
"You'll have plenty of chance."
"How come?"
"I think I'm going to scrap the play. It's dead wood. I could do something big with a character like Irma."
"I don't know what you see in her."
"She has a lot below the surface—like all icebergs."
"I wouldn't know. But I *do* know how you work—you'd have to see a lot of her before you could—what's your word?"
"Project her?"
"Yes. And if she's going right into training, you won't have much chance. It's a rugged life."
"Couldn't we persuade her to take a breathing spell before she starts in?"
"She sounded all set."
"She's had a dull life. If we make it attractive enough, I could study her in the process."
"Anything you say, sweet. But must she stay with us?"
"Wouldn't it be better?"
"For your purpose, maybe. But, honey, I hate sharing you."
"Nut! With a dream of beauty dished up to you like that! Just see *we* don't start sharing her."
"Baby, are those beans you're sticking up my nose?"
"Oh, Les, you're priceless," she said contentedly.
In the darkness, Lester politely stifled a yawn.

CHAPTER VIII

By the time Myra's breathing spell at the Hut was over, Irma Neves had settled her own affairs and was ready to shake the dust of her native village from her feet forever. When Myra and Lester drove back to town in Lester's flashy convertible, Irma sat between them. It was noteworthy that

Irma did not trouble to say good-by to a single soul in the village where she had spent her whole life.

The girl accepted her revised plans with composure. Her cool serenity was unbroken by the sight of Myra's delightful Sutton Place house; even the charming guest room with its huge picture window framing a view of the river, created no ripple on her placid surface. There was no apparent surprise that these strangers had so sweepingly adopted her, but neither was there anything offensive in her matter-of-fact acceptance of the situation. It was as if she understood why she was installed here and considered the bargain fair and agreeable, but no cause for gratitude. For a girl of twenty-two, with a background of narrow provincial life, she showed a remarkable aplomb. Myra could hardly wait to scratch her enameled surface. She was sure she would find more than mediocrity; nobody stupid could have drawn Irma's shrewd comparison between Hollywood and nursing as a field for operation.

Myra gave Irma time to unpack and settle in, while she sent for Eve to bring her up to date on professional affairs. Eve reported the various business items which had arisen during Myra's absence at the Hut. The picture contract for *Immoral Courage* had at last arrived, duly signed by the Hollywood moguls, together with the huge check. Miles Street had reported it over the phone.

Myra gave her a sharp look at mention of Miles Street but said nothing. She was beginning to wonder at Miles's frequent appearances at the Sutton Place house. Where he formerly restricted his visits almost solely to business agenda, he now showed up at all her cocktail parties and fished shamelessly for dinner invitations. The truth was not lost on Myra, and she did not relish the idea of losing a satisfactory secretary, no matter how excellent the match might be.

"What else?" she asked Eve.

There was a magnificent offer for the picture rights to an eleven-year-old short story of Myra's which some company scout had unearthed from a defunct magazine. The only catch to the offer was that Myra must agree to put it into scenario form, and as soon as possible.

"I thought delay might do the sale more good than harm, so I didn't relay it to the Hut," Eve explained.

"What story is it?"

"It's called 'Paint the Lily.'"

"Do you know, I can't recall a line of it."

"I dug a copy out of the files. It's good."

"I must read it at once. Anything else?"

"All the cylinders on the new play are transcribed. Your notes in one batch and the dialogue in script form."

"How does it read?"

"Well—" Eve hesitated.

"For heaven's sake, don't go gingerly on me, Eve!"

"It smells from herring," Eve blurted and awaited the storm.

"I know," said Myra amiably. "I'm scrapping it."

Eve stared. Finally she laughed and said, "I see. What's the *new* idea?"

"She's here in person." Myra gave a vivid word picture of Irma Neves. Eve listened intently and then sat quiet, turning it over in her mind.

"You don't think it's a little—sterile to sustain a three-act play?" she asked. "Without any emotional give and take?"

"I'm betting I strike oil deep down. A primitive like Irma is bound to have uninhibited appetites. Stack 'em up against her will to success and you get a good dramatic clash."

"Unpleasant, though."

"Since when, my good girl, do I write for commuters?"

"*Touché*. I'm beginning to see. It could be a lot more telling than *The Little Foxes*."

"Yes. And I shan't have to resort to murder—even passive murder. She will just leave havoc all round in her wake."

"When do I meet this Messalina?"

"Eve, you're dull today. Get the idea of deliberate wickedness right out of your head. She wouldn't hurt a fly if it didn't get her something. But if it did—she'd massacre without a backward glance. She's a force—like wind or tides. Even Les felt it."

"That's all to the good." Eve grinned. "Seeing she's so ravishing."

"Les is shrewder than you think. His instinct is sometimes sounder than all my word spinning. He says she gives him chills."

"She sounds really formidable. How did you induce her to put off her program?"

"Elementary, my dear Watson. I pointed out to her that money alone would pall in time. She should reach for position and power as well. And for that, she needs grooming—know-how, discrimination, even lessons in using the right forks, although socially she's quite presentable. She saw it at once. I could see her plans expanding in her mind."

"Was she grateful?"

"Not particularly. Hardly even curious. Although she did ask, 'What do you get out of it?'"

"That's hitting the bull's-eye. Did you tell her?"

"I said I liked helping people with drive."

"And that satisfied her?"

"She wasn't too interested. She's entirely concerned with Irma Neves."

"And you rig up a situation where *she* falls for someone else."

"My dear Eve, I don't rig up situations," said Myra sharply. "I watch her in action. I throw chances her way and let her meet the type that might stir her. I simply sit and record."

"Isn't it a bit tough on your men friends? Throwing them to this beautiful wolf?"

"Any man she'd go for would be strong enough to take care of his own hide."

"I suppose you know what you're doing," said Eve doubtfully.

"Oh, Eve, will you ever learn? How can I project her until I see what makes her tick?"

"And if she herself gets hurt?"

"Spare your qualms. Irma won't let Irma suffer."

"It seems to me that *somebody's* bound to suffer."

"My dear Cassandra," said Myra witheringly, "get it through your head that the labor pains involved in turning out a first-rate play are quite as demanding as in whelping a seven-pound infant."

"And God help the bystanders." Eve laughed.

CHAPTER IX

A week later Myra gave a cocktail party at which she introduced Irma casually and without explanation. She saw to it that the girl was effectively dressed by her own *couturier* and then left her to sink or swim alone. Irma swam. With some sixth sense, she by-passed the unimportant among the guests and concentrated on one or two of the unmistakably eligible. One of these, Harlan James III, a rather rabbity individual who ran to nearly a full page in *Who's Who*, was bowled over by Irma's radiance. Before the week was out, his Bostonian prudence went into eclipse, and he was rushing her with an impetuosity which was not long in reaching the ears of his mother on Beacon Hill. Meantime, he took Irma to the Stork Club, Twenty-One, and El Morocco, and smothered her in orchids.

Less to Myra's liking, was the effect Irma had on Steve Thatcher. The redheaded, slightly cynical Steve was not conspicuous for his continence, but his affairs had always had an air of triviality and transience. Irma seemed to have struck below this careless surface. For once, the redoubtable snarer was the ensnared. He lost his usual light touch with women and was awkwardly eager to please. He phoned her half a dozen times a day, gave an elaborate dinner in her honor at his penthouse, and neglected his office whenever Irma was free to hold sway in his box at the races. When the girl mentioned casually that she was afraid of wearing out her welcome at Myra's, Steve saw to it that a small apartment would become available to her anytime she liked in the Fifty-Seventh Street building which he owned.

It was no part of Myra's plans to have one of her real friends monopolized or hurt, but after a couple of weeks of uneasy watching, she realized there was nothing she could do about it but hope for the best. She dictated a few notes into her Dictaphone and made it her business to gather the reactions of her friends to Irma.

Edgar Van Roon thought her a delight to the eye but was

entirely impervious to her as an enchantress.

"I'm forty-two years old and a physician," he told Myra with a smile. "Handsome as she is, I can't forget that inside that pearly skin there are lungs, liver, and kidneys. I'm still looking for a heart."

Practically Lester's reaction, Myra reflected.

Miles Street's comment was short and dry. "Very attractive." To Eve, he was more outspoken. "On my word, I think Myra's utterly insane to throw that girl and Blaine together. She's crying for trouble."

"I don't think so," Eve replied. "Lester hardly looks at her."

"Well, if he was mad about her, even he wouldn't be senseless enough to show it."

"It isn't that," Eve said. "She's cold and stolid. She has nothing but her extraordinary beauty. And beauty to Lester, who's got more than his own share, is a drug on the market."

"The girl doesn't seem too popular with you, I note."

"I detest her," said Eve shortly.

"Any particular reason?"

"Yes. There was a nasty little incident here the other day. Irma missed a pair of earrings. Without rhyme or reason, she accused Lily, the colored maid, and as offensively as possible. Said all 'niggers' were thieves. For a minute, I thought Lily was going to hit her. I wouldn't have stopped her. I wish she had."

"What did Myra say?"

"She didn't know, and I persuaded Lily not to tell her. Perhaps I was wrong. Of course the earrings turned up. Irma offered Lily a dollar as a sop. Said 'niggers' had no feelings that cash wouldn't cure."

"And Lily?"

"She refused it with dignity. She said, 'Where I come from, a dollar ain't powerful enough to do all that work.' I could have kissed her."

"Very ugly, the whole thing. I wish Steve would get wise to her. Damn Myra and her writer's itch! He's too good to get hurt. And he's gone overboard about the girl."

"He may be overboard, but he knows how to swim."

"That has all the earmarks of an epigram. Better make a note of it," said Miles ironically. "I swear this house is just a nest of phrase makers."

"Don't worry about me," she returned. "I have no intention of sticking my friends on pins."

"Then what's this sharp pain I feel here?" He grinned as he put his hand over his heart.

"Better ask Doctor Van Roon," she said gravely.

"I'm asking you. I was hoping you had it, too, and we could swap symptoms."

"I feel wonderful, thanks," she said coolly. But a tide of color swept over her face.

He took her by the arms.

"From the vascular rush of hemoglobin to the cheeks," he said lightly, "I think you're a shocking little liar."

Among Myra's less intimate friends and acquaintances, Irma made a generally favorable impression. Accepted without question because of Myra's sponsorship, the girl's beauty was a minor sensation, and her stolidity, as Eve put it, was read as classic serenity. Tony and Alice Grier, longtime friends of Myra's, and social arbiters in their own right, put their seal of approval on Irma and invited her to their Eleventh Street house to dinner. The Douglas Masons, on the other hand, felt that the girl's beauty was too remarkable to be quite good taste and found nothing except her looks to recommend her. For Irma did very little to push her own claims beyond charming the eye. She was civil but static. She showed none of the pithy philosophy with which she had delighted Myra at the Hut. She seemed to feel that the wise thing to do was to sit back and let her looks do all the work. She kept her own counsel even with Myra, so that two weeks after launching her, Myra knew no more about her inner workings than when she first met her. The two happening to be alone one day at lunch, Myra finally did some delicate probing.

"From the look of things, Irma, we might save you the grind of hospital training."

"You mean I can marry Harlan James." It was a statement.

"It looks that way from the ringside. And he is eminently what you're after."

"I'd have thought so, back in Manhasset. Now I'm not so sure."

"Harlan's right out of the top drawer and certainly rich enough."

"I know. But there are drawbacks."

"Such as?"

"He's always been under his mother's thumb. As her daughter-in-law, I'd have a war on my hands."

"Yes, I think that's true," said Myra, marveling at the acumen of this inexperienced nobody. "But would you mind?"

"Why should I deliberately settle for second fiddle?"

"You might get a kick out of a polite battle. You've got a pretty extensive arsenal, you know."

"I have now. But as Mrs. Harlan James the third, I'd lose plenty of ammunition. Cleopatra herself wouldn't have a look-in against that Boston setup."

"Adelaide James is rather formidable. She's always ruled the clan with a rod of platinum. How did you discover it so fast?"

"From her remote control of Harlan. She's got him buffaloed. He's dying to take me to Boston to meet her but he always turns tail at the last minute."

"Well, if not Harlan?"

"There's Steve Thatcher, of course," said Irma.

"Don't set too much store on Steve. He's hardly the marrying kind," said Myra, hoping to throw cold water on this project.

"You're wrong there. He's begging for it."

"Really?"

"But I'm not having any."

"You *are* getting choosy, my dear."

"I've seen enough of drunkenness to last me a lifetime."

"Nonsense! Steve's convivial but—"

"My father was convivial at Steve's age. He ended up as an A-one souse."

"Well, with Harlan and Steve in the discard, have you any other prospects?"

"After *all*, Mrs. Blaine! It's only been three weeks."

"You're right, of course. You've really done wonders in the time."

"I've made a good start. Of course, as your friend, I'm traveling without any lead in the saddle. As a nurse, I won't be. There'll be the element of lifting me out of the basement."

"You'll be the death of me, child, with your uncanny wisdom."

"Canny, you mean, don't you?"

"Perhaps. Well, we'll see what a few more weeks will bring forth."

"I've been underfoot here long enough."

"Nonsense."

"Steve's getting me a little apartment in his building."

"But, my dear, I don't want you to leave, I *like* you around."

"Oh, you'll see plenty of me. If you'll just keep on asking me to your parties and taking me with you, now and then, until I'm sort of established on my own, I'll be all set."

"But of course. And it might be a good move. If you need any money—"

"Thanks, no."

"One thing, Irma. Pay your own rent. Don't let Steve—"

"Absolutely. Things like that get around."

"But can you run to it?"

"Oh, yes. I've got fifty-two hundred dollars now. It's a different pair of shoes getting tips on the horses from Steve. Well, I must run. He's taking me to Belmont, and it's past one."

She rose. Myra watched her lovely, long-legged stride as she crossed the room. At the door she turned and said guilelessly, "This would make a good scene in a play, wouldn't it?"

Myra sat, a puzzled frown on her face. Below the guilelessness, she seemed to detect a sullen resentment.

CHAPTER X

Myra, rereading her eleven-year-old short story, "Paint the Lily," found it still fresh and interesting. With the Irma situation more or less static, she fell to with a will, turning the story into a workable scenario, piling up cylinder after cylinder of dictation for Eve to transcribe. It was her custom, when working intensively, to forego most social distractions, dividing her day into three periods—work, physical exercise, and rest. She did, however, remember her promised obligation to Irma and spoke to Lester about it one morning over their breakfast trays in her bedroom. Breakfast in bed was an inviolable habit of theirs, Lester performing a prescribed ritual which never changed. While Austin raised the Venetian blinds and sorted out the trays, Lester piled pillows behind Myra's head, lifted her bodily to a comfortable position, and kissed her hands in morning greeting. When Austin, with a wooden face which hid any inward mocking he may have felt, set Myra's tray across her lap, Lester, with the air of an acolyte, poured her coffee and creamed and sugared it with painstaking care. Only then did he turn to his own tray.

Myra sipped her coffee, and ran through her mail, laying aside business communications for Eve and glancing through personal letters. Three of these she tossed across to Lester.

"Look, dear. Here are three invitations I can't possibly make."

"Okay, sweet. We'll send regrets," he returned promptly and cheerfully.

"The thing is, I've rather got Irma on my mind. I've done practically nothing for her since she moved."

"I'll say you've done plenty for her."

"Well—I promised I'd take her about with me here and there." She smiled. "After all, she's got to be seen to be appreciated."

"Still bent on sticking some guy with her?"

"Still trying to find the type of man who could rouse her."

"No such animal. The lady has White Rock in her veins, honey."

"I'm betting you're wrong. But my point is—now I've launched her, I've a sort of obligation to go on with it."

"Well, can't you make an exception and go to these shindigs?"

"I *am* making some exceptions—we're going to Steve's dinner tomorrow. But Alice's cocktail party and this Tod Lucas opening tonight—I just am not up to them after a hard day's work."

"As I said, let's pass 'em up."

"I thought if you'd go without me—and squire Irma—"

"What good would it do her to go out with a married man? It might even hurt her."

"Darling, come out of the McKinley era. It would be a load off my mind. I'm really working at top speed these days, so that we can get out of town soon."

"And about time, too, darling. You shouldn't drive yourself the way you do."

"I'm tough. If you'd just take Irma off my hands, I could go through my usual schedule and be fine. Work in the morning, some hard golf this afternoon, and dinner on a tray in bed."

"When you put it like that, sweet, of course I'll do it. But I'll be glad when this damn scenario's finished and you remember you're my wife again. Nothing's any fun without you, baby."

Relieved, Myra worked steadily all that morning. Her study was a big air-cooled, soundproof room, sparsely but comfortably furnished with a desk, a few shabby easy chairs, a couch and dozens of ash trays. Its most formidable feature was the big Dictaphone which Myra had had made to her own specifications some years before. She was a restless worker and did most of her dictation on her feet. It irked her to have to sit in one spot in order to talk through the mouthpiece of the regulation Dictaphone, pressing and releasing its button. Consequently, she had consulted with the company's engineer, suggesting some revolutionary changes. He had agreed that it was possible to tap the main cable of the machine and string a series of microphones throughout the room, which could pick up her voice wherever her perambulations might take her.

"But, Miss Hudson," the engineer had said (this was years before her marriage), "it's sheer waste to do away with the button. When you stop to think or light a cigarette, you'll be using up space on the cylinder that you'd save if you just snapped off the button. Then, when you want to start actual dictation, you just press it on and there you are, all set to record."

"How can I think or compose?" she objected. "All my attention would be centered on your damned little button."

"You're the doctor," he had shrugged. "But you realize you're simply turning the whole room into a sending-station, rigged for recording. This thing will be no more a Dictaphone than Studio A at WNBC."

"Fine! How long will it take you?"

The cost had been exorbitant, but the results were satisfactory. The engineer had also contrived an ingenious arrangement whereby she could adjust a dozen cylinders into the machine which automatically succeeded one another on the spindle and slipped off into a padded trough when they were full. It was similar to the action of a self-changing phonograph and saved Myra from interruption when she was in full swing.

There was something of the actress in Myra, as there must be in any competent writer of plays, and some of her most effective scenes were accomplished as she strode up and down, assuming the role, now of one, now of another of her characters. The effect would have struck an onlooker as comic, with this five-foot-two wisp of a woman portraying a six-foot hero. But there were never any onlookers. It was a Median law that between the hours of 9 a.m. and 1 p.m., nothing less than a fire was sufficient cause for anyone to pass the portals of the study. There was no phone in the room, and its soundproofing isolated it from the rest of the house.

Around half past twelve, Myra began to slow down. Her lines of dialogue were interspersed with irritable phrases.

"No! Cut that." "That's rotten! Go back to the start of the scene," etc.

Wisely, she realized she was written out for the day and stopped work. She left the study and went to find Lester.

Lily, the pretty, light-tan parlor maid, told her that Mr. Blaine had gone off early to Forest Hills, leaving word that he would be back around five. Lily added that Mr. Street had just arrived and was waiting in the living room.

Myra found Eve with him, a fact she did not altogether relish. More and more, it looked to Myra that she was in danger of losing the most intelligent secretary she had ever had.

Miles explained that he had brought some papers which required Myra's signature. Her lips curved satirically.

"The service of Street, Wyatt, and Street is improving. I can remember the days when all transactions had to take place in the Broad Street offices. Today, I can rely on a member of the firm appearing on my doorstep at the drop of a contract."

Miles laughed. "We strive to please," he said mildly.

Myra shrugged and signed where he indicated.

"Now you're here, I'll give you lunch if you play hooky for the rest of the day. I need a tough round of golf this afternoon."

"Very glad to oblige," he returned. "Provided it's over before midnight. I'm catching the twelve-o'clock plane to Washington tonight."

"That should be possible. I don't envy you in this heat. Washington will be a furnace."

"Oh, I'll be back Thursday morning. Which reminds me, Myra, Friday's the Fourth of July, making a long weekend. My people have invited Eve down to Southampton for it. The traffic will be bad, so if you'd let her off early Thursday afternoon, we could make it before the rush starts."

"Certainly, Miles," retorted Myra, bittersweetly. "Nothing I like better than to be left high and dry in the middle of a tough chore of writing."

"I won't leave you high and dry, Mrs. Blaine," Eve put in stiffly. "I can drive myself down in the Ford on Friday."

"Oh, no you won't, Eve," said Miles. "If this Simon Legree doesn't let you off, I'll beat the tar out of her this afternoon on the links. She'll be ashamed to show her face at Green Hollow again."

"You bully!" Myra sighed exaggeratedly. "Very well, I'll be a martyr. Only is it in a good cause? Eve, I advise you to think twice before you tangle with this blackmailing ruffian."

"Thinking seems to do no good at all," said Eve resignedly.

At lunch, they talked of public events, of the deplorable standstill in the progress of world unity, of conditions home and abroad, and of the place the theater should have in molding public opinion. But back in the living room after lunch, as they drank their coffee, Miles broached a new topic.

"Myra, I want to talk to you as a friend as well as a lawyer."

"Something unpleasant, of course, with such an opening," she smiled wryly.

"I'm serious. And I'd be grateful for a cooperative hearing. If you'll just stop being a spoiled child for ten minutes—"

"Well, Miles!" She raised her eyebrows. "It *must* be serious. Go on, I promise my earnest attention."

"It's this. You're forty-three years old—"

"Really, Miles—"

"And the last of an old and honored family. In all likelihood, you won't have children. Even the Hudson name is submerged since your marriage. Are you going to let it be totally forgotten?"

"Perhaps my plays may survive me by a few years," she murmured.

"Yes, I think that's true," he returned thoughtfully. "But I believe you should do more."

"Miles, are we, by any chance, back on the subject of my will?"

"We are, Myra. I think you are doing a preposterous, a vicious thing in leaving the Hudson fortune unconditionally to a man like Blaine."

"To my husband," she retorted, too quietly.

"Myra," he urged patiently, "we'll grant Blaine is a thoroughly upright chap, a good husband and deserving. But face other facts. His origins are pathetically meager and poverty-stricken. Nothing against him, but not a background conducive to the judicious handling of a tremendous fortune. With all his charm and good nature, you must admit he's hardly an intellectual giant. With complete control, what's he going to make of such an inheritance?"

"I don't care too deeply," she replied, now as serious as Miles himself. "He's given me something invaluable. No amount of money is too much to repay that."

"He's fifteen years younger than you. What if he marries again?"

To his surprise, almost embarrassment, Myra's face was flooded with a dull brick-red, as she cried sharply, "No! He couldn't do that!" It was a revealing, painful glimpse into her possessive soul. Eve looked away, uncomfortably. But Miles followed up his advantage inexorably.

"Why not? When you're seventy, he'll be fifty-five. With twelve million dollars back of him—to say nothing of his looks—he'll still be a prize for any woman."

Myra did not answer. She set down her coffee cup, lit a cigarette, and began to prowl up and down the room. Miles was wise enough to say no more, and Eve was past speaking. She would have given much to get out of the room gracefully. The pause began to grow strained.

Suddenly Myra turned to Eve and said harshly, "Get your book. I want you to take some notes."

When Eve returned with a notebook, Myra went on in a hard, repressed tone.

"You'll have your wish, Miles. Eve, put this down. The whole Hudson fortune plus all future royalties and revenues from my work—picture sales, radio rights, television, and so on—will be formed into a trust fund, from which the total income will go to Lester. Got that?"

Eve nodded.

"On one condition," Myra snapped.

Both Eve and Miles raised their heads and looked at her.

"In the event of Lester's remarriage at any time whatsoever, he forfeits every penny of income from any and all sources of my estate."

"That's very unwise, Myra. He's entitled to something," Miles exclaimed.

Myra ignored him.

Eve scribbled, Miles puffed at his pipe, and Myra continued to prowl up and down the room. Minutes later, she went on.

"If, when, and as Lester remarries, the estate shall be used to establish the Myra Hudson—not Blaine—Myra Hudson Foundation for young writers. The Rhinebeck farm will be turned into a colony where gifted young people will be given a chance to learn, study, and exercise the art of writing. They will be supported until they begin to earn through their work. They will be selected on the recommendations of editors, theatrical producers, college English professors, and a committee who will judge from scripts submitted directly to the foundation by the writers themselves. The details of the foundation can be worked out later. I want the new will executed as soon as you come back from Washington—well, after your weekend—but no later than Monday. Eve, make a transcript of those notes this afternoon and leave them in my study. I shall want to include a few minor legacies and personal effects—to Edgar, Steve, and you two. Miles, if you're ready for

Green Hollow, so am I."

During the drive up to the country club, through the afternoon of hard golf and the drive back to town, no word was said about Myra's will. In spite of her declaration to Lester that morning that she would dine off a tray in bed, Miles induced her to go to a small, as yet undiscovered, Swedish restaurant where the smorgasbord was a saga.

Over their dessert, Miles asked, "And how is the great Irma experiment?"

"Marching with banners, from her angle. She's got two of my best bachelors eating out of her hand. In fact, it looks so easy to her, she's beginning to be choosy."

"There's a good side light for you. The insatiability of the ambitious."

"Could be. Just now I'm taking soundings for heart."

"Heart! Are you kidding?"

"Well, desire—passion—avidity—I don't care what you call it. But something that would switch her off—conflict with the main offensive."

"Going a bit Pinero, aren't you? Strikes me that's the line *any* writer would take with this material."

Myra gasped.

"Good Lord, Miles! You're right! Am I slipping?"

"No. But I think you're glamorized by her looks. You're mistaking her beauty for drama."

"No, she's got force. There's something galvanic about her that has nothing to do with her looks."

"Okay. Use it. Take away her beauty. Motor accident. Smallpox. I don't care what—that's *your* job. Then see how she makes out with her force, her galvanism, and so on. That *would* make a play."

"Pay the bill, Miles, I've got to get home."

"I thought you had strict rules about working hours."

"Rules can be broken. You've opened up a lode of pay dirt. I won't sleep until I get down a few notes."

When Miles dropped her at her door, she found the house silent and dark. Lester, she knew, was at the Tod Lucas premiere with Irma. Mrs. Link, the cook, and Lily, the maid, slept out. Austin, whose room and bath adjoined the kitchen, was not in evidence. Either he was out or had already retired. She liked the feel of the quiet, empty house. She felt ready to do her best work and wondered if the night hours were better than her usual morning time for work. She went straight to the study and closed the door. Eagerly, she adjusted a dozen cylinders into place.

Smoking furiously, lighting one cigarette from the end of another, she marched up and down, pouring out a steady flow of crisp, illuminating phrases, like actual nuggets from the lode. Miles's meager suggestion broadened into a fertile concrete outline, interspersed with brilliant snatches of dialogue. Not once did she have to use the crippling "No—cut that." She was like a machine herself, or a violin, spilling faultless melody from a living source. Time ceased to be, her surroundings were invisible, she was unaware even of herself in the sweeping flight of pure creation.

At midnight, practically out on her feet, she staggered, bemused and exhausted, up to bed, forgetting even to turn off the lights or the Dictaphone.

CHAPTER XI

After eight hours of dreamless sleep, Myra woke up, completely rested. She had never felt better in her life. The memory of last night's effort flooded her mind like a bath. She exuded energy and satisfaction at every pore. She could hardly wait to review her work with the critical ear of the morning after. Without a qualm, she shoved the scenario job into the background and looked forward with gusto to expanding the notes on the Irma Neves theme. She was bursting with whole pages of dialogue that screamed to be written.

Lester, looking handsome and fresh in black-and-gold pajamas, came in at the same time as the breakfast trays. After the usual ritual of pillow-plumping and hand-kissing, he tipped up her face.

"You look wonderful this morning, honey. If rest does that to you, I'm glad I took over your chores."

"You're sweet, Les. How was it last night?"

"The show was poison—the usual June opening. Irma and I—and half the audience—left after the second act. We went to some bar for a drink afterward with the Griers, and then Irma and I stopped in here for a cheese sandwich before I took her home."

"Glad I gave it a miss."

"You should be. When we came in around twelve, I thought we had burglars. Your study door was open and the lights on full blast."

"I must have left them. I went down there for a minute."

She carefully hid the fact that she had broken her rigid routine of working only in the mornings. Lester would have spent the rest of breakfast time, lovingly reproaching her. Hurriedly, she switched the subject.

"Meet anybody worth Irma's while?"

"If I were a girl, I'd think so. I don't know about Irma."

"Who was it?"

"Bart Stanton, that Wall Street boy wonder they're all talking about. Alice Grier introduced him. He smoked a cigarette with us in the lobby after the first act and seemed quite taken with Irma. But as far as I could see, she didn't give him a tumble. You'll have to go some, to find a guy who'll open *her* pores."

"Well, it doesn't matter. I've got a new slant for the play. If you're finished, run along like a good boy and let me dress. I've got a big morning's work ahead of me."

"You bet you. But it's so darned swell, this breakfast hour with you, I always waste your time like nobody's business."

He kissed her and made for the door, where he turned and added, "There wouldn't be a part for yours truly in the play, by any chance?"

"Oh, Les, still harping on that string?"

"After all, I *am* an actor."

"You *were*, darling. You're my husband now."

"Couldn't I be both? If you wrote in a fat bit just suited to my style—I'm not asking for a star part—"

"I don't write that way," she said curtly.

"Of course, I don't mean to hurt the script—but if it so

happened—if it fitted— It would be fun to be on Broadway again—maybe even featured."

"Look, Les. Suppose I did. Just at the time of day when *I'm* free and want you with me, you'd be tied up at the theater. No sense to that."

"I just thought I'd ask. It's okay, sweet. The hell with it, if it interferes with us being together. Sorry I brought it up again."

"That's a good boy. Scram now, darling. It's nearly nine."

After a quick shower, Myra slipped into a smock and sandals and shut herself up in the study. Les, Irma, the house, her whole life fell away from her.

She adjusted the Dictaphone for a playback of last night's work. Her world centered on the spinning cylinders. For an hour she sat, motionless, spellbound, a mere ear, a receptacle for sound. When her recorded voice finally ceased and the needle purred almost silently on the cylinder, she stretched luxuriously, her little eyes alight with devotion to her work.

"That's *good*," she whispered exultantly. "Alive. Sharp. On the mark." She reached for a cigarette, lighted it, and sat for a few moments, smoking and planning. Then she saw that the cylinder was still spinning and rose to click off the playback switch. As her hand neared the switch, the purring of the needle gave place to a voice again. More dialogue was coming from the cylinder. And not in Myra's voice. She stood, her hand arrested above the switch, turned to marble stillness

When the last cylinder slipped off the spindle and dropped silently into the padded trough, Myra groped blindly to the adjoining bathroom and was violently sick.

CHAPTER XII

At just about the same time, Irma, delightful-looking in a green-checked gingham, was busy putting her little apartment in order. Her golden hair was tied back with a green ribbon, giving her a more girlish look than usual.

Her bell rang, and she opened the door with a pleased expectancy. Nearly every morning, on his way down from his penthouse, Steve Thatcher rang her ground floor bell. And nearly every morning, Jimmy, the elevator boy stood behind him, loaded with some pleasant surprise "loan" as Steve called it. The whole apartment was furnished with selections from Steve's own apartment, which he tendered with such grace that Irma could hardly have refused them even if she had wanted to. One morning it was a curly-maple set of chairs and table for her breakfast nook. Another day, it was an Italian credenza of exquisite silky wood, for her living room. Once it was a rose-and-blue Saruk rug that was very nearly a museum piece.

"You'll be doing me a favor if you let me stash this down here," he said. "The sun pours in up in my place all day long and it's just about ruining this rug."

The rug practically made Irma's living room.

Today he had a variety of offerings. There was an exquisite Wedgwood bowl, its tiny Greek figures sharp against the soft blue. There was a case of Haig and Haig Pinch bottles.

"In case," Steve said impishly, "I'm thirsty some evening when I'm collecting the rent."

And finally, there was a small, beautifully made, blue-steel .22 automatic, which, as it lay in Steve's big palm, didn't look nearly as deadly as it was.

"Can you shoot?" he asked her.

"I used to be quite good at it. In Manhasset, we used to pepper tin cans until they looked like sieves. But what do I want with it here?"

"Well, I worry a bit about you down here on the ground floor. Just as soon as I can, I'll see to it that you get an apartment higher up."

"Steve, how ridiculous! In a big building like this. And with Jimmy and the doorman right outside."

"I know but the neighborhood's none too good—Avenue A and First Avenue. Lots of hoodlums around. And with your separate entrance on the street. Jimmy, you can put that case in the kitchen."

"Yes, Mr. Thatcher. That sure is a pretty little heater," the elevator boy said, eyeing the automatic as he shouldered the Haig and Haig.

"Put it in a safe place, Irma. And don't be careless with it. It's loaded."

"I wish you'd take it away, I'm sure I'll never have the least use for it."

"Well, if you keep it, *I'll* feel more easy in my mind. A girl alone—"

"I'll be alone plenty when I'm a nurse—both indoors and out."

Jimmy, richer by Steve's tip, went back to his elevator. Steve laid a hand on her arm.

"Forget that rot about nursing, Irma. That's no life for you." She moved away from his hand as if it irked her to be touched.

"If you know anybody who'll endow a poor young orphan," she said lightly.

"*I'll* endow you—with my name and everything else I've got. I'm looking for the chance."

"Thanks, Steve. Not right after breakfast."

"At night you say it's too late to be serious. Now it's too soon after breakfast. When the devil *will* you listen to me?"

"If at all," she put in, lightly.

"Now look here, you young fiend. Are you just trying to key me up tighter, or don't I measure up to your standards? You know, I'm not such a worm financially or socially. In fact, they tell me I'm a damned good catch. What's wrong with me?"

"Maybe it's wrong with *me*."

"I'll take a chance—Irma—" His mocking voice deepened with feeling.

"No, Steve, not now. Please. Go on to your office. You keep abominable hours. When do you get any work done? It's nearly ten now, and if we're leaving for Jamaica at one—"

"Three hours is a long time for a brainy guy like me." He grinned.

"Well, *I've* got work to do. Please run along."

"I'll go if you kiss me good-by."

"I'll do nothing of the sort," she said curtly.

"I wonder about you, Irma," he said slowly. "You're so gorgeous, so lush, so made for love. At least you *look* it. What are you really like?"

"Ask Myra," she retorted. "She's making an intensive study

of the subject."

"And you don't like it, do you?" he asked shrewdly.

"Not particularly. But if it gives her any pleasure—" She shrugged.

"*I* wanted to know for a different reason. I'd like to wake you up, Irma."

"Thanks, I'm wide-awake now."

"Hopeless." He sighed plaintively. He stuck his Panama on the back of his red head and prepared to leave.

"Oh, Steve, about tonight."

"Tonight?"

"Your dinner—"

"Well? Don't you dare tell me you're not coming."

"Oh, no! I'm looking forward to it. I just had a suggestion to make."

"Anything you say will be given our earnest consideration."

"It's so warm, I thought it would be nice if we dined on the terrace."

"It's really cooler inside with the air conditioning."

"But it's so lovely outdoors, high above the city—"

"God bless us, she has sensibilities after all!"

"Oh, stop it, Steve!" She bit her lip, annoyed.

"Sorry, my sweet. Of course. On the terrace, along with the East River soot and the Manhattan mosquitoes. See you at one."

CHAPTER XIII

Myra, pale, shaken, but deadly calm, groped her way back into the study. Her legs felt like rubber beneath her, but she forced them to carry her back to the Dictaphone. With trembling hands, she took the last three cylinders out of the trough and adjusted them again in the machine. She clicked on the playback switch, sank into a chair, and listened to the records again. She heard the final lines she herself had dictated the night before, the short blank, of perhaps three or four minutes, while the cylinder spun almost noiselessly, and then the voices of Irma and Lester.

IRMA: She must be around with all these lights on.
LESTER: She isn't. She's in bed. She said she was going at seven. She even had her dinner in bed.
IRMA: Then why is it all lit up?
LESTER: Austin, probably. Forgot and walked out.
IRMA: Well, I don't like it much.
LESTER: I'll close the door. There. Now it's absolutely soundproof. And it's the coolest spot in the house.
IRMA: I still don't like it—
LESTER: Well, you wouldn't let me come to your place.
IRMA: It's much too risky. Steve's in and out as if my apartment was Grand Central.
LESTER: I wish you'd drop him, Irma. I go wild when he acts like he owns you.
IRMA: Nobody owns me, Les. And don't worry about Steve. He's just somebody who might do me some good.
LESTER: How can he do you any good unless you—
IRMA: Marry him? Well, if the worst comes to the worst and you and I can't work out some plan, maybe I will marry him.
LESTER: Irma! Don't talk like that even in fun.
IRMA: It's not fun, Les.
LESTER: Darling, I can't stand it! If you did that, I'd go out of my head—
IRMA: But Les, I've got to do something. And soon. My few dollars are melting away. If I don't grab this chance to get in the money—
LESTER: Irma, you'll drive me crazy, talking that way. You *couldn't* marry anybody else!
IRMA: *You* did.
LESTER: But I hadn't met *you*. It wasn't so bad, then. A nice soft berth. Handing her a line. Making with the mush stuff. Kissing her little yellow cheek. It paid off fine. But now—I can't eat, I can't sleep. It's as if I'd been dead all my life and now suddenly I'm alive—and mad for you—I can't trust myself anymore—
IRMA: Which reminds me. I want the key back you took out of my desk.
LESTER: Don't worry, darling, I promised I wouldn't use it till

you let me.

IRMA: I know, but in the state you're in—some night you'll take a chance—I won't have it.

LESTER: If you loved me enough, you would.

IRMA: You know I love you, Les. It's only for your sake I'm so careful.

LESTER: *My* sake?

IRMA: Yes, your sake. Do you realize what she'd do if she found out?

LESTER: All right, she'd divorce me. That'd be swell with me. Then you and I—

IRMA: You're sweet, Les. I love you when you're romantic.

LESTER: Who could help it with you?

IRMA: Fine. Be as romantic as you want about *me* but don't be romantic about money.

LESTER: Money?

IRMA: That's what I said. Let's face facts. You and I are a lot alike. We both love nice things, luxuries, easy money. Right?

LESTER: Sure. I guess so.

IRMA: I know I do. I swear, Les, if I thought I'd have to drudge all my life at nursing or something, I think I'd kill myself. Life wouldn't be worth living. And you're no different.

LESTER: If I had you, I wouldn't care—

IRMA: Don't kid yourself, honey. Suppose you told her point-blank about us—

LESTER: If you'd only let me!

IRMA: She'd be wild. You're her *property*.

LESTER: So what?

IRMA: She's proud, Les. It would kill her to be thrown over. She'd take it out on you.

LESTER: What could she do?

IRMA: She'd have you blacklisted in every theater in the country. She could do it, too.

LESTER: Then I'd take some other job.

IRMA: She'd hound you down, whatever you did.

LESTER: She's not God, exactly.

IRMA: She thinks she is. And at that, she's pretty powerful—rich and famous—she could do plenty.

LESTER: There are other places. We could get out of town.

IRMA: Suppose we did. You take a job for fifty a week in a garage. How would you like that after the life you've had with her? Cars, butlers, clothes, swanky clubs—you have to admit she's free with money.

LESTER: Well, I earn it, don't I? Giving up my career, playing errand boy, licking her shoes—

IRMA: The thing is, what would you do *without* those things, now you're used to them?

LESTER: If only—

IRMA: I know what you're going to say— If only something would happen to her.

LESTER: I meant—

IRMA: She'd deserve it, too. All she thinks of is herself. Other people are just worms for her to step on. Look what she's doing to me—nosing into my business, watching the wheels go round, sticking me under the microscope like some kind of a bug instead of a human being. And why? So she can do a play out of me. So everybody will rave about her brains and her brilliance and kowtow to her.

LESTER: No joke.

IRMA: And you. Parading you around like a prize bull, bossing you, never giving you a chance in one of her plays—just slowly murdering you, squeezing the life out of you—

LESTER: Y'know, that's true.

IRMA: And here we are, young, full of life, we love each other— we've got a *right* to be together. And just because one old, selfish, cold-blooded woman stands in our way— But what's the use? She'll probably live till she's eighty.

LESTER: What I was going to say, if I could get her to give me a decent lump sum—hey, Irma, don't touch those things. She goes nuts if anyone handles her papers—

IRMA: Hm?

LESTER: —We could light out and laugh at her. But try and get it. Oh, no! She doles out my allowance every month like you give a kid at school— What's that you're reading? After all, I'm her husband. I'm entitled to a real share of her money *now*. Irma, listen to me. Just because she's provided for my future— Irma, what's so funny? What good is it if I have to wait years and years— Irma, have you gone crazy? What are you laughing at?

IRMA: Here! Here! Read this! *Read* it! You *bet* she's provided for your future—

LESTER: What on earth?

IRMA: Read it!

LESTER: I—don't get it—

IRMA: Don't you? Don't you? Isn't it plain enough? "In the event of Lester's remarriage at any time whatsoever, he forfeits every penny of income from any and all sources of my estate." Oh, yes, she's provided for your future, all right!

LESTER: The bitch! To do that to me, after I've sacrificed my youth and looks and talent to an old hag like her!

IRMA: I told you what she was. Keeping you tied to her all your life and then doing you dirt in the end.

LESTER: To play a rotten trick like that!

IRMA: *Nothing's* too bad for her.

LESTER. You're right. I'll get her for this!

IRMA: I don't blame you.

LESTER: I'll make her pay for it—

IRMA: Oh, Les, I know what you're thinking of—

LESTER: If it's the last thing I do, I'll get even—

IRMA: And I admire you for it.

LESTER: Admire me?

IRMA: She *deserves* to die—

LESTER: *Die?*

IRMA: Darling, you're a *man!* Most people would rant and rage and then do nothing about it. But you! Oh, Les, you're wonderful! Strong and cool and daring—

LESTER: But Irma—I didn't m—

IRMA: It makes me so proud of you—

LESTER: Listen, Irma—

IRMA: And I'll show you, I can be just as brave. I'll *help* you.

LESTER: *Help* me?

IRMA: To think you love me enough to risk your life for me!

LESTER: NOW, look, Irma—

IRMA: Darling, it'll be so wonderful—we'll be together. And

soon, *soon*. It's just Providence we found this paper—
LESTER: I know, Irma, but—
IRMA: We'll travel—we'll be rich—we'll have each other—
LESTER: Oh, darling, when you talk like that, I can't wait. Only—
IRMA: I know exactly how you feel; when you want something, you *go* for it. If something's in your way, you ride over it. If it happens to be people, you ride over *them*.
LESTER: Irma! You really feel that way about me?
IRMA: If you only knew how I feel!
LESTER: It's true; *she* does deserve to die—
IRMA: Most people would be shocked. But we're above that. *We* know that life's the cheapest thing in the world in wartime. Why not in peacetime?
LESTER: You're so thrilling, Irma! Whatever you say is right. When I'm with you, I can do anything!
IRMA: Of course you can. Now, honey, we've got to be practical. This paper is a sort of rough draft. There's a note at the bottom. "Attention, Mr. Miles Street, July 7th." Do you see?
LESTER: Just what—
IRMA: There isn't any new will—yet. There won't be until July 7th. That's Monday. After Monday, you're out—unless you stay single all your life, and even then, you can't touch her money, only the income.
LESTER: The rat!
IRMA: But *until* Monday you're still her heir under the will you told me about.
LESTER: Yes. Well?
IRMA: If she should die *before* Monday—
LESTER: I get it.
IRMA: You'd be her heir without any trust funds, without any conditions, without any strings to twelve million dollars.
LESTER: That's marvelous. But won't it be awfully risky? How can we do it?
IRMA: We'll work out a way together.
LESTER: We'd never get away with it. As her heir, I'll be suspected before she's cold.
IRMA: Not if it's done right.

LESTER: That guy, Street. He's smart as a steel trap.

IRMA: We'll be smarter.

LESTER: You don't know how tough it is these days. If you shoot somebody, they can tell it just by examining your hands. I read about it. They call it the paraffin test.

IRMA: Who's talking about shooting?

LESTER: What then?

IRMA: Well, when I sold my father's office, I took a couple of items out of his cabinet. You'd be surprised at some of the *medicines* dentists use.

LESTER: You mean—*poison?*

IRMA: I don't mean tooth powder.

LESTER: But how would we know how much—how to—

IRMA: Don't worry about *that*.

LESTER: You talk like you *know*.

IRMA: I know, all right.

LESTER: *She* told me once—some question about your father's—

IRMA: Never mind about my father!

LESTER: You needn't be afraid to tell *me*, darling. We're in this together. You can trust me.

IRMA: Well, if you must know, there *were* a few questions—

LESTER: Was there an autopsy?

IRMA: Certainly not.

LESTER: Did they suspect you?

IRMA: Of course not. It was just routine. Now, forget about my father. What's important now is how to give *her* poison. We've got barely a week.

LESTER: It'd be different with her.

IRMA: Different? What are you talking about?

LESTER: Poison's no good.

IRMA: What's wrong with it?

LESTER: She's as tough as nails. Never sick. And all of a sudden going off like that. It wouldn't be just a few routine questions. She's a big shot.

IRMA: That's true—

LESTER: And Street's smart, as I said. He hates me, too—looks at me like I was a slug that crawled out from under a rock—

IRMA: You're right.
LESTER: And that Doctor Van Roon—he'd come nosing around and spot it—
IRMA: Les! You're so clever! What would I do without you?
LESTER: It won't work, Irma.
IRMA: Of course it'll work. But it can't be poison or a gun or a knife. You're absolutely right.
LESTER: What then?
IRMA: Don't you see? It's got to look like an accident.
LESTER: You've got it.
IRMA: An accident—a simple innocent little accident—something foolproof—

The last cylinder rolled off the spindle and dropped softly into the trough. The playback switch clicked off automatically.

CHAPTER XIV

Myra's first reaction was a blind, overpowering rage. She literally shook with fury against both Lester and Irma. She pounded her small fists upon the solid oak desk until they were bruised, in the subconscious urge to batter the two traitors to a jelly. Her breath came in sobbing inarticulate little cries which sounded more animal than human. Kaleidoscopic images floated before her mind—of skulls cracking under a bludgeon, of faces smashed to a pulp, of blood gushing in streams. The paroxysm was so violent it drove the blood from her head and heart. The room whirled, then blackened, and she slid unconscious to the floor.

After a long time, she stirred, shuddered, and sat up dizzily. She stared about her wonderingly. Then it all came flooding back to her. She crawled to an easy chair and lay back, fighting her weakness, before facing this monstrous nightmare.

When her feet were able to carry her, she staggered to the liquor cabinet and took a long pull from the bottle, her teeth chattering against the glass like castanets. Back in her armchair, she waited while the whisky quickened her pulse and revived her reason. At last she found herself weak but normal and in full command of her thoughts. The blind rage gave way to a cold, implacable hate. She saw Lester for what he was, a paltry, treacherous pimp, and burned with shame that she had really loved anything so shabby. Her clear mind did not spare herself. She jeered, "No fool like an old fool," and wanted to tear herself to pieces in self-abasement. How right Miles had been and what a fatuous figure of fun *she* had been to swallow whole Lester's oily flattery and paid-for kisses. How blind she had been, too. There had been plenty of signposts pointing to what he was. The elderly woman, for example, whom he had cajoled into bringing him to New York and financing him for a year. His chagrin when she died without remembering him in her will. Even the army, which he liked because he could sponge on the government for his support. He hadn't even been smart enough to hide these evidences of his real nature. But she, Myra Hudson, the proud, the clever, the understanding, had ignored the glaring truth because his sea-blue eyes, his charming smile, his magnificent body had blinded her to everything below the surface. He was almost too small to hate, too abject, too chicken-hearted. He was an insect, a cockroach to be exterminated by the scuff of a shoe.

Irma was different. To begin with, she owed her life to Myra. At some risk to herself, she had saved the girl from sure death by drowning. She had wanted no thanks but neither did she expect so vile and vicious a return. It was true that she had befriended Irma for her own purposes, but she was doing her no harm by studying her actions and reactions and, in return, she had more than evened the score. She had seen to it that Irma was exquisitely dressed for her new role and had footed the bill. She had taken her into her home as a guest and had introduced her to people she could never have met otherwise. She had placed her in a position to make a brilliant marriage which was the epitome of Irma's ambition. However, as Irma had told her, Harlan James and Steve Thatcher, her two conquests to date, had drawbacks. Also, while they were both wealthy men, their fortunes were paltry compared to Myra's. With the weak, infatuated Lester as an instrument, Irma saw herself in complete control of twelve million dollars.

With a bitter grimace, Myra remembered a snatch of her talk with Eve. Eve had said that a play about Irma could be more telling than *The Little Foxes*. And Myra had replied, "Yes. And I shan't have to resort to even passive murder. She could just leave havoc all round in her wake."

Instinctively, Myra had sensed the girl's possibilities for evil, but to the one-sided mind of a playwright, Irma had been just so much interesting material. She had ignored the human element, and Irma had, indeed, left havoc all round in her wake.

Nothing was bad enough for such a snake. Lester she would simply divorce and throw out on his ear. A playback of the cylinders in any court would clinch it—

She stopped dead. Never, under any imaginable circumstances, could she let that damning dialogue become public property. She could never survive being the laughingstock, the butt of the hidden smirks or the expressed condolences of the world. Her social status, her wealth, and her talent had given her a position at the top of the ladder for so long, that she could only breathe the rarified air at the top. That air contained vanity, egotism, and arrogance, which were as vital to her as the oxygen in it. Without them, she couldn't—or wouldn't—live.

She would talk it over with Miles—

Again she shied like an unbroken colt. Not even to Miles, who knew so much about her, could she unburden this hideous thing. She could not bear to read the "I told you so" in his eyes, which he would be too tactful to voice.

She ran over a list of her intimates in her mind. Edgar Van Roon. Steve Thatcher. Alice Grier. Lotta Mason. Eve Taylor. To no one of them could she endure to expose her nakedness.

And these were her friends. She shuddered as she saw herself as her enemies must have seen her from the first—a fatuous, ugly woman, verging on middle age, desperately snatching at her lost youth, much as one would try out a new vitamin. How had her penetration and good judgment so deserted her, that she could have swallowed the nauseating drafts of Lester's flattery? How could she have dreamed that this young, handsome, ignorant nonentity could have found anything attractive in her? Her brain, her complex and keen intellect—her only asset—must have repelled rather than drawn him, showing him up, as it must have, for what he was. And yet, looking back, she marveled how he had played his part. She could remember no single instance where he had slipped up in his lines. He was a better actor off stage than he ever was on. From his angle, he had indeed earned what he received, as he had said.

But she would fool him. She would cut him out of her will altogether— Again she pulled up short. If she cut Lester out of her will now—after she had admitted to Miles and Eve only yesterday that she loved him—Miles would guess instantly that she had discovered Lester in some infidelity. Searing phrases such as "May and December," "Beauty and the Beast," "Fool's Paradise" crossed her mind. They would cross Miles's mind, too—and the mind of her whole world. She could not bear it. Whatever revenge she took on Lester, he must still be playing the adoring husband when he was cast into outer darkness.

The same stumbling block held in Irma's case. She had, of course, a deadly weapon to hold over the girl's head—the undoubted fact that she had murdered her father, which could be easily proved on investigation. But that, again, entailed the publishing of the dialogue on the cylinders. It was definitely out. Whatever Myra decided on, in the way of punishment, Irma must still be, ostensibly, her protégée, her friend, the girl whose life she had saved. It would take some thinking about.

She felt a certain artistic exhilaration in the circumstances. It was an issue to be resolved, a crisis to be licked. She was in a favorable position. Like the gods of Olympus, she knew *their* plans while—

Suddenly, devastatingly, for the first time it hit her, what their plans were. *She was slated to die.* These two diabolic criminals planned to murder her in cold blood, in order to snatch her money. Even now, they were probably working out their "foolproof" method.

Well, she would turn the tables. Singlehanded, she would beat them to the draw. She had complete justification; she must destroy them both, before they destroyed her.

The crisis became a duel.

CHAPTER XV

The clock on the desk said half past eleven. Not three hours since she had entered the study to savor the satisfaction of reviewing her work of last night. She had a sudden, immense distaste for writing. Fiction paled to the aspect of a child's preoccupation with blocks. She had real work to do.

Up and down the room she paced, reviewing the known facts before attacking the problem itself. First of all, they had decided that crude slaughter, by gun, knife, or poison was too risky. Myra was an important person. Her sudden death would cause a sensation. There would be much more than the casual scrutiny which had been given Irma's father. Intensive investigation would train a spotlight on every circumstance surrounding her death. Besides public inquiry, Edgar Van Roon, prominent as a physician and utterly devoted to Myra, would study the facts with a microscope. Steve Thatcher, wise in criminal lore, could smell a murder a mile off. And Miles Street, her lawyer, jealous for her rights and property, had always suspected the worst of Lester. It was exceedingly shrewd of Lester and Irma to decide that the thing must look like an accident. Whatever the quality of their intellects, in the matter of crime they were dangerous opponents and worthy of respect.

They had decided against the use of poison. But Irma had poison in her possession, she had undoubtedly used it once successfully and they had less than a week to contrive her death. Their plans for an accident might prove infeasible, and in the long run, they might revert, in desperation, to poison, after all. At any rate, she would take no chances. She must be careful of every bite of food, of every swallow of liquid which passed her lips. She must be watchful of every vitamin pill she took, and of the sleeping tablets she occasionally resorted to, when she was wakeful. How easy to introduce a deadly dose into the innocent bottle.

She thought of her breakfast, brought up by Austin every morning. How natural, if Lester contrived to meet him at the top of the stairs and suggested carrying her tray in, himself. Actually, he had done so a few times, so that it would cause no surprise or suspicion. A quick motion and her coffee or orange juice would become a lethal draft.

But, somehow, she did not believe it would happen that way. Lester was a timid and reluctant partner in the plot; he would share the loot gladly, but he would shy at being the active perpetrator of the deed. Being, as he had said, the prime suspect in case of her unnatural death, he would see to it, with his superficial cunning, that he had an excellent alibi for the time of the crime. Myra honestly felt that her moment of greatest danger would be at a moment when Lester was miles away, leaving death behind him in some unguessed form.

Besides, it struck her that Irma, by far the stronger of the two, would hardly trust him to carry it out alone. Despite Irma's avowal that she loved Lester, Myra could hear her contempt for him in the whole dialogue on the cylinders. She would see to it that Lester was equally involved in the murder with herself, but she would rely on herself alone for the efficient execution of the crime.

Recalling Irma's callous philosophy about the cheapness of human life, it occurred to Myra that the girl might even find a macabre relish in murder itself, that she might consider it a more thrilling adventure than a night with any man. The more she considered Irma, the more she was convinced that the girl had a definite pathologic taint.

Having resolved to go warily where food and drink were concerned, Myra next considered the matter of accidents. She put herself in their place. If she were planning a fatal accident, what form would she devise? The most obvious was, of course, a motorcar accident. They both knew that Myra drove her Chrysler fast and daringly. And the car stood in the private garage behind the house, along with Eve's Ford and Lester's Cadillac. How simple to tamper with the steering gear or some important internal part which would give way at high speed and dash her to destruction. She made a note to phone the service station to call for her car for a complete overhauling. This would keep it out of their reach, at least until after the deadline, July seventh. Also, she would do no motoring with Lester in his car. She could picture a situation where she could be killed and he come through, unscathed but still innocent appearing.

Golf was positively taboo. Lester was an excellent golfer and might very possibly encompass a fatal blow with a golf ball or even with a club itself. He might be called criminally careless but he could never be convicted of murder.

There was the matter of a fall, arranged to look accidental. She would stay away from the windows and high places religiously. She recalled a fantastic trick in a crime play she had once seen. The murderer had strung a bit of wire across the third or fourth step of a flight of stairs. The victim had tripped and crashed to his death at the bottom. The murderer had instantly removed the wire and there was no evidence at all that it was anything but an accident. Myra resolved to go downstairs holding firmly to the banister. She would feel her way to every step before she took it.

The one danger that nearly drove her to a panic-stricken appeal for protection was fear of smothering. Lester was immeasurably stronger than she was. Suppose in the night he crept into her room and held a pillow relentlessly over her face until she suffocated. Her outcries would be muffled, and she would writhe helplessly until she was dead. She could, of course, lock her bedroom door but that would rouse his suspicions. And if she were to accomplish his destruction and Irma's, they must not dream that their intended victim was at work. In the end, she borrowed a leaf from the crime play. She would stretch a cord across her bedroom door and tie it around the body of a vase nearby. When the door was opened the vase would be jerked to the floor and shatter noisily, and she would be warned. She hoped to be able to awaken in the morning before Austin arrived with breakfast, so that she could remove the cord. If she did not, she must chance that it would appear to be a mere accidental crash. But it could not happen a second time without causing speculation. She saw that she would have to act fast, much faster than her opponents. She could not afford as remote a deadline as July seventh.

A bathtub misadventure was out. There, at least, she could protect herself by lock and key. The only other thing she could think of was fire, and that appeared too uncertain in its effect for them to attempt. The house was fireproof, and if a fire was set in her room, she had only to rush to the balcony outside her window, to be safe until her cries brought help.

As things stood, she felt reasonably safe. Forewarned was much more than half the battle. Knowing her danger, she could sidestep it. It was, of course, a gamble but she decided it was worth it. She was risking her life to save her face and to mete out jungle justice.

She must, of course, treat them both precisely as usual. She must accept Lester's kisses and solicitude with the exact mixture of affection and patronage she had always shown him. She must be just as lavish with money toward him, and at the same time, as demanding on his time and service as ever. With Irma it would be quite easy. She was seeing very little of the girl these days and when she did, she could preserve the smooth enamel of her friendliness without obvious effort.

The ground cleared, she must now plan her counter-offensive. It was not easy. Lester must be destroyed, but at his death there must be no breath of suspicion against Myra, and he must still figure as the devoted husband to the end.

Again, the stock motor accident idea, with, this time, Lester and Irma as victims, appeared a simple solution. But it did not satisfy her. First, because she knew too little of the inner workings of a car to be sure she could manage it successfully. Second, she felt that swift destruction was not punishment enough for Irma. For a long time she pondered the question—what would Irma consider a worse fate even than death?

At last it came to her, the perfect scheme. But what a problem it was! It had more cogs and interacting parts than a seventeen-jewel watch. She choked down her personal feelings and became the competent craftsman. Myra Blaine, the wife, disappeared before Myra Hudson, the playwright. She attacked the matter in the cold professional style that she used in dramatic construction.

She sat at her desk and pulled a writing-pad toward her.

Lester, Irma, and herself became A, B, and C. She began jotting down facts, motives, opportunity and time schedules. She discarded infeasible methods and built necessary steps toward feasible ones. She cleared away obstacles and developed expedients and procedures. She moved Irma and Lester around like a couple of chessmen. She made notes of what she had to do and how she must do it. By half past one, she had the clear beginnings of a path which would lead to the desired goal. The one thing she did not yet have was the method by which Lester must meet his death. Her mind went round and round like a squirrel in a cage, but she could not decide.

She put her notes in an ashtray and set fire to them. She even burned the top blank page of the pad, in case any tracings from her pencil showed through. She flushed the ashes down the drain and left the study.

She sent for Eve and told her not to touch any of the cylinders in the Dictaphone trough.

"I've fallen down somewhere in the scene," she explained to Eve. "And I want to play them back before you do any transcribing. Leave them just where they are."

Up in her room, Myra looked into her mirror and was shocked at her haggard face. She wondered if the harrowing experience she had gone through was responsible for the change or if there was no change except that she was seeing herself as she really was, for the first time.

Well, the world must see as little as possible. At Steve Thatcher's dinner tonight, she must be as serenely self-assured as usual. She reached for the phone and called her masseuse.

CHAPTER XVI

Steve's dinner was for eight. Besides himself, Irma, Myra, and Lester, there were Tony and Alice Grier, and Douglas and Lotta Mason. Steve's duplex penthouse apartment was alight from top to bottom when Myra and Lester arrived. The others were already there, Irma, breathtaking in filmy white, the older women in darker but equally summery clothes. Steve was occupied with a cocktail shaker as big as a samovar.

"Just on time, Myra," he called across the forty-foot living room. "These things are like omelets. No good if they stand."

Myra smiled, but her thoughts were not amusing. In the time it took her to cross the room, she was arguing at a furious rate. Could she accept a drink with safety? She saw that Irma was beside Steve and could possibly have tampered with the contents of the shaker. But even though it was known and accepted that she never took a drink herself, would Irma dare to poison the whole company in order to accomplish Myra's death? She thought not. Then a real solution crossed her mind. She would delay tasting her drink while she watched Lester. If he drank his, she could safely do likewise.

She paused in her trip across the room to exchange greetings with Alice Grier and Lotta Mason. The three women had been at school and college together, and their intimacy was one of common memories and background. Alice was a pretty, plump little woman, surprisingly untouched by the years, guileless and eager to please. Lotta was tall, dignified, and humorless, with a strong sense of her own importance. Her husband was the owner of a powerful chain of distinctly conservative newspapers and took himself as seriously as his wife. Tony Grier, on the other hand, took only yachting and horse racing seriously.

"Myra, dear," Lotta pronounced tactlessly after their greetings. "You're overworking again. I can see it by your strained, abstracted look."

"Nonsense, Lotta," Alice put in. "She looks wonderful. It's only that that new Schiaparelli chartreuse is a frightfully difficult shade. Most women couldn't wear it at all. I know I couldn't."

"Lotta's right," Myra said pleasantly. "Only it's not overwork. It's this wretched, sticky heat."

"I can't think why you're still in town," said Lotta. "*I've* got to stay because Douglas has this important conference coming up next week and I feel I ought to be with him. But you—"

"I suppose I must confess. I *am* doing a rush job for Hollywood. And it *has* taken the starch out of me a bit."

She watched Steve's Cuban butler offer his tray of drinks to Lester, who took one and immediately drank it down.

"I'm in the same boat as Lotta," said Alice. "Tony positively refuses to leave town until his sloop for the Marblehead races is ready. And the poor boy is helpless without me."

"Martyrs, all of us," said Myra lightly. She took a drink from the butler along with the others. Then, paving the way for her future conduct, she added, "How silly of us to touch alcohol when it's so hot. This is positively the last drink I'm going to touch tonight."

"We ought all to do the same," said Alice. "Otherwise you'll have an enormous advantage over us at bridge, with you sober and the rest of us full of Steve's powerful concoctions. Oh, while I think of it. Thursday's Tony's birthday. I'd like to surprise him with a little dinner and bridge party. Can you both come?"

Myra, casting back over the hours that morning in her study, decided that Thursday, July third, fitted very well into her complicated plan. It was a bit soon, but the sooner the better for her own safety, and if she worked fast, she thought she could be ready in time.

"I'm having just this same crowd," Alice went on. "I've already asked Steve and Irma. And be sure not to give it away to Tony."

Myra strolled over to Steve who was sampling his third dividend from the bottomless shaker.

"Hello, Steve—Irma—" Myra greeted them. "How did the horses treat you today?"

"Irma's a millionaire," groaned Steve. "I, like a fool, refused to put my trust in a tip on a two-year-old maiden. But she had a bundle on it, and cashed in at the beguiling price of $59.60. What did you win, Miss Croesus?"

"Plenty," said Irma complacently. "Enough to indulge myself in that white satin Schiaparelli showed last week."

"Sounds very bridal," said Myra.

"No, it's severe. Pure Greek. You'll see. I'll wear it to Alice Grier's Thursday night."

"A dozen Schiaparellis couldn't cost what you won today," Steve said. "I hope you put it in a safe place."

"You ought to build in wall safes for your tenants," Irma returned. "Then you'd stop worrying." She turned directly to Myra. "Is he always such a fussbudget? Do you know, he actually presented me with a loaded gun this morning for my protection."

"Steve, what a charming attention to your Dulcinea!" said Myra with a high, exaggerated laugh. Inwardly her heart slipped its beat so violently that the room reeled. *Irma had a gun!* What incredible, magnificent luck! The one point in her elaborate scheme which she had been unable to bring into line. All morning long, she had been irked by the means by which to exterminate Lester. She had turned over idea after idea, only to discard them all. The closest she had come to a decision had been a plan to abstract some of the poison which Irma had said she possessed. But she was dissatisfied with that solution. The poison would not be easy to come by, and even if she obtained it, it was not the ideal agent for the climax which she had planned. But a gun! The gods must be with her to provide this perfect answer to her problem—and not only to provide it, but to inform her at the crucial moment, when she could make use of the knowledge.

Irma's voice seeped through her whirling thoughts like an echo.

"Well, please take the thing away, Steve. Didn't anybody ever tell you that there's such a thing as the Sullivan law? And you failed to provide a license."

"All right, all right—" Steve was interrupted by his butler, announcing that dinner was served.

Myra was burning with excitement. Did Steve's "all right" mean that he would take back the gun or provide Irma with a license? In any case, she herself must act with terrific speed. If only she could manage tonight to slip downstairs to Irma's place—but of course she couldn't get in—yet. Her furious thoughts batted against her brain like moths against an arc light.

Suddenly she froze.

Steve, taking her arm, was saying lightly, "... dinner on the terrace. Irma thought it would be nice."

"But it's so much cooler indoors," Myra managed to say.

"Just what I told her. But she insisted. Romantic of her, isn't it?"

Romantic! Myra almost laughed that the astute Steve could be so dense, that he could let himself play cat's-paw to Irma's murderous schemes. For it shone out like a light why Irma wanted them to dine on the terrace, twenty-two stories above ground with only a three-foot parapet between Myra and a dash to the street below.

Well, she was on guard. She shivered as she remembered that if she had not forgotten last night, in her weary, bemused state, to turn off the Dictaphone, she would be totally unaware of their ghastly intentions. How easily and unsuspiciously she would have paced the terrace with either Irma or Lester, laying herself open to a sudden fatal push, out of sight of the other guests.

But circumstances, destiny, the gods, whatever one cared to call it, were on her side. She was forewarned, she was in complete control of the situation, all she had to do was to be careful, to keep well away from the parapet, to stay with the others, in order to frustrate their cold-blooded design.

Steve's quarters covered the whole roof. The terrace, about twenty feet wide, was carpeted in some sort of plastic grass, which, together with the plants, flowers, and low trees in tubs, gave a charming imitation of a country garden. Swinging couches, deck chairs, small umbrella-topped tables, and a perpetually playing fountain to cool the air, made it as comfortable as it was attractive.

The dinner table, gleaming white under the soft candlelight, was set on the south terrace. All of lower Manhattan spread before them in the blue darkness, cut across by the narrow, lighted tapes which were streets, and the broader ribbons of the rivers, east and west.

The dinner was informal, without place cards. Myra, on Steve's arm was the first on the terrace. She lost no time in taking a seat with her back to the penthouse. She sat at Steve's right, while Irma, facing her, sat at his left, therefore with her back to the lovely panorama. With a curl of her lip, Myra thought how stupid Irma was. She had insisted to Steve on dining outdoors for the sake of the view, and then, illogically, forgot to carry out her pose by turning her back to it. She herself would be guilty of no such inconsistencies, any more than she would have allowed a character in one of her plays to behave incongruously.

Her thoughts ran in a clear, direct river, purposeful and definite. She knew now exactly where she was going, what she was going to do, and how she was going to do it. There were one or two extremely difficult points to overcome, points which a less determined person might call impossible of achievement. But Myra felt suddenly like a giant refreshed, capable of anything. The news of Irma's gun had acted like a shot of adrenaline on her. Not only did it complete her plan, but the fact that she had so opportunely learned it just when she needed it most filled her with a sense of supreme power. Her luck was in. Nothing could stop her.

Steve's chaffing voice broke in on her reverie.

"Well, Myra, that clears up your Act Two curtain, I'm sure."

"Steve! Forgive me." She laughed. "You're not far wrong. I *did* just resolve a ticklish situation that's been bothering me."

"Darling," Lester put in. "You're at a dinner party. Remember? Work's *verboten*."

"Artists can't help where ideas are born," Steve told him. "Any more than imminent mothers who have their babies in taxis."

"You might tell us about it, Mrs. Blaine," said Irma. "From your expression, it looks exciting."

"It is, rather. At least, to me. When it's all worked out, I'll let you see what you think of it."

"How anyone can think in this heat," said Lester. "It's criminal the way you drive yourself, dear, when we ought to be away, taking it easy."

"We will, Les, dear. A few more days and then—I promise you—nothing but rest." She thought it a neat bit of phrasing.

The bridge tables were set up on the terrace, on the west side, where whatever breeze there was, came from. Before they settled down to the game, Irma strolled around the terrace with Alice. When she reappeared, she said to Myra with much more animation than usual, "Myra! You must look! You can see your house from the east side of the terrace. It looks adorable. Like a tiny doll's house. You must see it."

"I know. I've seen it before," she returned dryly.

They took their places at the tables, Mason, Steve, Alice, and Myra, a really expert foursome; the others, less adept, at the second table.

The two games progressed for an hour without incident. Myra put her mind to the game, deliberately excluding thoughts of anything but bridge. Then, behind her, Lester's voice came, saccharine as ever, but bringing a chill to her heart.

"Darling, Mrs. Mason told me you weren't drinking any of Steve's heating brews tonight, so I asked Perez to make you a plain old-fashioned lemonade." He deposited a tall frosted glass on a coaster at her elbow.

"That was sweet of you," she said with stiff lips. "But you should know by now that I hate soft drinks."

He looked dashed, disappointed out of all proportion to the occasion.

Alice said, "Leave it here. Lemonade sounds a good idea."

"Of course," said Lester. He took up the glass to carry it around the table to Alice. There was a soft crash and an exclamation. The glass had slipped out of his hand onto the plastic-grass floor. "Oh, how clumsy of me!"

"No harm done," said Steve. "Blaine, as long as you're dummy, would you tell Perez to make a pitcherful?"

Lester nodded and walked away. But the little incident had unnerved Myra. Her game deteriorated rapidly. She constantly asked to review the bidding; she took unreasonable finesses; and finally, in a redoubled hand, she threw the game by reneging. Only the fact that she was holding phenomenal cards kept her on the winning side.

Then the second incident occurred. She was playing with Steve, she sitting with her back to the penthouse, Steve on the parapet side. Steve was playing a hand, leaving Myra, as dummy, free to move around. There was a small table beside Steve on which lay Myra's and Alice's evening bags. Myra wanted her handkerchief. Instinctively she glanced at the other table before she rose. Lester was playing intently, and Irma, obviously dummy at their table, was nowhere in sight. Myra walked around the table and had just opened her bag, when she felt an arm slipped through hers and someone impelled her urgently along. They were a few paces away when Irma's voice came, quiet but insistent.

"Myra! Quick! Don't upset the others. But I think there's a fire at your house. You can see it from the east side."

Myra pulled back, but Irma still urged her forward. "Nonsense! You're dreaming, Irma!"

"No, really. I mean it. Come and see for yourself."

They were around the corner now, on the south side, out of sight of the others. Irma was almost running her along, and she realized how strong the girl was. Then suddenly, from one of the French windows, Perez appeared with a tray of drinks. Irma slowed down, and Myra was able to jerk away from her.

"Let it burn!" she said with a breathless laugh. "I hate the old place. Always have. Steve's playing a four-spade doubled. That's much more important!" She sped back to the table, panting as if she had been in a race.

"Made it!" Steve announced to her triumphantly. "Myra! What's up? You're as pale as a ghost."

"Irma gave me a shock. She thought for a minute my house was on fire."

Irma appeared, serene, smiling, apologetic.

"I'm an idiot, Myra," she said. "It was the reflection of a gas flareup in Long Island City. It's already out."

Coolly, she went back to her table.

The evening was it finally over. Myra and Lester walked the short block to her house through the warm deserted street.

"You looked wonderful tonight, sweet," he told her.

"You see it does you good to get out. All work and no play—"

"How right you are. I'm glad I went."

"And why wouldn't you be? *You* won forty-two dollars. I wasn't so lucky." There was a faint trace of petulance in his voice.

"You're not short, are you, dear?"

"We-ell—"

"Oh, Les, I wish you'd come out with these things. *I* don't know how far your allowance reaches, if you don't tell me."

"I hate always to be asking you—"

"That's ridiculous. I've got much more than I can spend and you know whatever I have is yours."

"My sweet, generous girl."

"Remind me to increase your allowance tomorrow."

"Thanks, honey. That'll be a big help."

"But, Les, it wouldn't do you any harm to study that new bridge manual."

"Oh, my bridge is sound enough," he said defensively. "It's the foul cards I hold. Well, who cares? Unlucky at cards, lucky in love."

As the clichés tripped from his lips, Myra wondered how she could ever have been so asinine as to love him. Even if his lovemaking had been sincere, how had she overlooked the fact that he was a crashing bore? Had she been so hungry for flattery? Had she reached the nauseating period of life when some women hanker for the physical caresses of a young handsome male? Her contempt for her own blindness sickened her. But she answered him softly.

"Darling, what would I do without you?"

At home, he wandered in and out of her room as usual, while he undressed, dropping his tie here, his coat there in the process. On one of the occasions when he strolled across the hall to his own rooms, she darted swiftly to his coat and dropped it behind an armchair where it was hidden.

When he came back in his shorts, his tanned shoulders and chest almost insolent in their young strength, she looked at him, no longer with the admiration that was his due, but with the calculating thought that forty-eight hours from now, that firm, healthy torso would be food for worms.

But she shook off these mental excursions. As he idled about the room, now fiddling with the big crystal cigarette box on her table, now picking up her hand mirror, she watched him vigilantly, especially when he wandered near her bed table on which stood a water carafe, a box of sleeping tablets, a bottle of vitamins, and a pack of cigarettes. Any one of them was vulnerable to attack, susceptible of being tampered with. But he never came close enough to the bed table to touch anything, and as far as she could judge, had nothing on his mind except the banal small talk that flowed so readily.

At last he kissed her and left her for the night. She would have given much to lock her door, but she dared not. She must make no move which might alert them.

Until she struck, she must appear to be the easy victim, the marked-down prey.

Instead, she carried out her plan borrowed from the crime play. She took a long length of heavy white cotton thread, secured it to one side of the door with a thumbtack, carried it across the door to an adjacent chest of drawers on which stood a tall jar of flowers and wound it round and round the body of the jar. The opening of the door would bear on the thread until the jar was dragged forward and down with a crash that could not fail to awaken her. On the bed table, she placed in readiness a stiletto-sharp letter opener, the only weapon she could devise at the moment. If Lester should come in to smother her in the night, a few sharp, painful thrusts might give her time to elude him and get out of the room to safety.

She picked up his dinner coat and went through the pockets. Sure enough, in the right outer pocket was his tiny alligator key case. There were five keys suspended from the small silver rings. Two were obviously car keys, to the transmission and trunk compartment of his Cadillac. One she recognized as the house key, identical with her own. The fourth was a long flat one marked *Green Hollow Country Club*, the key to his locker. The fifth one set her heart beating with excitement. It was a house key, slightly different from the other house key. Was it the key to which Irma had referred? The key that would make all her plans possible? The key to safety and revenge?

In her mind's eye she pictured the little apartment Steve had secured for Irma in the building he owned. It was a ground-floor apartment, obviously meant for a physician because it had one entrance directly from the street—maisonettes, she believed they were called. It could also be entered from the lobby of the building, but on the occasion of Myra's one visit to it, Irma had humorously declared that she would reserve the door to the lobby solely to let one lover out, if a second one rang the street doorbell.

"It's the sort of thing bad playwrights devise," Myra had answered lightly. "To get their characters on and off stage. Cain's Warehouse used to be full of just such settings."

She stood, now, the key case in her hand, considering. She was tempted to detach the single key and try it on Irma's door when feasible. But Les would notice his loss and probably tell Irma. It would set Irma thinking, and that was bad. Instead, she took the whole key case and hid it under her mattress. If she could not return it to Les before he missed it, it was better that he should believe he had lost the whole key case rather than this one particular key off its tiny but secure ring.

She put out the light and got into bed, shrinking at the darkness and at her supine helpless position in the bed, fearing desperately that sleep might prove to be her greatest enemy. She need not have worried. She watched the dim yellow glow from the street slowly whiten to the summer dawn without ever slipping off into a moment's oblivion. Around seven o'clock, she removed the thread from the door and went back to bed to await the day.

CHAPTER XVII

Lester was already in her bedroom when Austin brought in the breakfast trays. Lester behaved exactly as usual, going through his routine of hand kissing, pillow adjusting, and coffee pouring. She never took her eyes off his hands, but there was absolutely nothing suspicious to see.

She had a good-sized check ready for him and bore his grateful lovemaking with a set smile.

"Any plans for today?" she asked at the first pause.

"It's a bit cooler today. I thought I might get in some golf."

"I rather wanted you to do something for me."

"Just say the word, honey. To hell with the club."

"You spoil me, Les. There's a Napoleon snuffbox going on sale this morning at Parke-Bernet. I simply can't get away. Could you go and bid on it for me?"

"Surest thing."

"It's a little gem, part of the Harriet Gale collection. I'll go as high as five hundred for it."

"I don't know beans about those things but won't it bring a lot more if it's so perfect?"

"You never know. I've picked up finer ones for less, and then again, I've seen inferior ones bring much more. It just depends on who's bidding." She did not add that she wanted him sitting in the auction rooms, solely to keep him out of the way and at a place where he would not need to use either his car or locker keys that morning.

As soon as he was out of the house, she sent for Eve and gave her a job of research work which would keep her at the public library most of the day. Eve was shrewd and observant. The less she saw of Myra's activities today and tomorrow, the less she would have to remember when she was questioned later.

Eve out of the way, Myra went into Lester's room and opened his desk. Although he seldom wrote a letter, there was a formidable array of stationery, heavily engraved with his name and the Sutton Place address. There were letterheads, postcards, notecards, and pads with envelopes of every size. Carefully, using a handkerchief as a shield, Myra selected a pad and carried it back to her room where she dropped it on her own desk.

Then she went up to the trunk room in the attic. Years before, she had joined a summer stock company for a season, in the belief that one could write better for the stage after actual experience on it. She had been right, and it had helped her considerably. Myra Hudson plays were eminently actable. She still had the properties of that summer session in an old trunk and after a ten-minute search, came downstairs with a box of grease paints and a handsome blond wig.

She put on an inconspicuous black linen dress, dropped the wig and a pair of dark glasses into a capacious handbag, and watched her chance to leave the house unobserved. Mrs. Link, the cook, was no problem. She rarely left the kitchen. Lily, the pretty chambermaid could be heard down the hall, humming "A-huggin' and A-chalkin'" as she straightened Eve's room. Myra stole downstairs, reconnoitering. The rumble of Austin's voice and the clatter of metal told her that he was polishing the silver in the pantry. She slipped out of the house.

She walked to Bloomingdale's, made her way to the women's rest room, retired to the privacy of a pay toilet, and emerged wearing the blond wig and dark glasses.

She took a crosstown bus, then another uptown on Amsterdam Avenue. In the Eighties, she got off and walked until she found a hardware store, which displayed a sign *Keys Made*.

The twenty-five minutes during which she waited for a duplicate of the strange house key to be made, seemed the longest of her life. She stood, her back to the door, staring at an assortment of sink brushes and mousetraps, her mind busy with the many details of her plan still to be accomplished. At last the key was finished. She paid the stout German salesman a quarter and left. She thought it highly improbable that at any future date, he could connect the blond customer with Myra Blaine.

Again she detoured, this time, to the ladies' room of a busy Fifty-Seventh Street hotel, emerging minus wig and glasses. When she reached home, she let herself in softly, hoping to escape notice. If Austin or Lily met her coming in, she had a word of explanation ready, to account for her being out during the sacred work hours of her day. But the entrance hall and stairs were deserted, and she reached her room unobserved. She hid the blond wig in a bureau drawer which she locked. She put the fifth key back in Lester's key case, restored the case to his dinner-coat pocket, and hung the coat in his dressing room closet. The sight of the dozens of beautifully tailored suits, the long row of handmade shoes for every occasion brought a bitter smile to her lips. She wondered who would wear that splendid sartorial array after tomorrow.

Back in her room, she called Irma on the phone, inviting her to a private art show that afternoon. Again she smiled wryly, practically certain of Irma's response. But she had to know the girl's plans for the afternoon. Irma declined. But Myra, with acrid amusement, could interpret the long pause before she actually refused. She could almost hear the girl debating with herself the chances of an accident in a crowded art gallery or in the taxi going or coming back. Apparently she decided against it and said with polite regret, "I'd have loved it, but I'm booked again for Jamaica with Steve."

"At the rate you're going," Myra returned lightly, "your quest for a rich husband won't be necessary. The horses will feather your nest without human aid."

"Oh, I don't always win," Irma said.

"Did you get the Schiaparelli?"

"I ordered it. It'll be ready to try on tomorrow afternoon."

"You'll have good use for it at Newport. I ought to be ready to leave by next week. Get yourself something special in the way of bathing suits. We spend a lot of time on the beach."

She actually heard Irma suppress a giggle.

"I'll do that."

"Well, until tomorrow night—"

A glance in her mirror showed her that the combination of the heat of the day and the pressure of the wig had taken the wave out of her short, grizzled hair. It was positively lank, and she told herself that she had never looked plainer in her life. She called Francine and made an appointment for four o'clock.

She decided, for her own purposes, to lunch with Lester. She wanted to keep informed of his movements for the day and to arrange for their evening together. If possible, he and Irma must be kept apart until tomorrow night.

For the first time since her marriage, she did not care if she looked a fright or not, in his presence. Grimly she told herself that that was, indeed, the measure of how out of love with him she had fallen overnight.

She came into the dining room just as he entered it from the pantry door. He had been in the kitchen and when he saw Myra, he explained why—rather too elaborately, it seemed to her sensitive ears.

"Darling! You're just in time. Austin's got hold of some magnificent stone crabs at the market. I've just told Mrs. Link how to fix them the New England way."

"Sounds wonderful, dear, but I don't feel up to them in this heat."

As Austin brought in their chilled Madrilene, she pushed it away and added, "Austin, will you tell Mrs. Link to poach a couple of eggs?"

For the life of her, she couldn't tell whether Lester's face fell from guilty disappointment or if he were just acting the usual solicitous husband.

"Did you get the snuffbox?" she asked him.

"It went for eleven-fifty. Howard Regan got it."

"Well, it doesn't matter. Sorry I ruined your morning."

"Doesn't matter, sweet. I can get in eighteen holes this afternoon. Why don't you come with me?"

"With this stringy hair?"

"What on earth did you do to it?"

"Oh, just the humidity. That's the curse of women with straight hair. Sometimes I feel I could kill Irma for her indestructible natural waves."

"She has got nice hair—if you like blondes."

"Don't all men?"

"Not me. Too much of a towhead, myself. I like 'em dark and interesting, like you."

"Silly. I was talking to Irma just now on the phone. I wanted to take her somewhere with me, but she's going to the races again with Steve."

Again, her hypersensitive ear caught the uncertain pause before he replied. She was sure he was wondering why Irma had passed up an afternoon with Myra, which might have afforded some possibility. Then he said naturally, "Y'know, honey, I think we can ease up on giving Irma a boost. Looks to me like she's picked on Steve, poor devil."

"Why poor devil?"

"How many times must I tell you, baby, a man doesn't just marry a *face?* A wife's got to have more than Irma can offer."

"I never could understand your rabid dislike of her."

"Hey, don't get me wrong. I don't dislike her a bit. She just gives me chills."

"Bunk! Under that serene mask, I'll bet she's a very hot number."

"Darling, no woman ever read another woman right. Believe

me when I tell you, the guy who picks Irma has bought himself a hunk of dry ice."

As Myra spooned up her insipid poached eggs—which she resented, as she liked good food—she told herself again that she must be careful not to underestimate Lester. Stupid he was, from a cultural angle, but his attitude of mild indifference to Irma's charms, which he had shown from their first meeting four weeks ago, had been consistently maintained and never overplayed. Knowing the wild passion which this pose concealed, she realized that, chicken-hearted or not, he was a formidable antagonist. Unpalatable though they were, the poached eggs were a wise move.

After lunch, she heard him in his room, changing his clothes, whistling "I Got Plenty o' Nuthin'" lightheartedly. It was a favorite tune of his. Evidently he had located his key case in his dinner coat pocket, for he made no inquiries. He looked into her room, in the swankiest of golf togs, to kiss her good-by.

"Darling, tuck your silly hair in a net and come along," he begged. "Nothing's fun without you."

She could hardly control the churning of her stomach at his smooth lies. Then it occurred to her that he might indeed want her on the golf course with him, more than anything in the world. A well-directed blow would pay him enormous dividends.

"I'd love it," she said, smiling. "But we're going to Ray Meredith's cocktail party. If I don't get a hairdo, I'll scare the citizens."

"Okay. Then I'll make it my business to be back by six."

"Yes. We can go on from Ray's and dine some place cool." Again there was that telling pause, which she read as frustration of any plan to be with Irma. Then his face lit up so eagerly as he agreed, that she decided to pick up a couple of people at Ray Meredith's and carry them off to dinner. Dining *à deux* seemed much too much to Lester's taste.

She heard him start the Cadillac and roar out of the garage but she waited a full half-hour before she set out on her own errand. Just before she left the house, she dialed Irma's number. There was no answer.

CHAPTER XVIII

As she walked the short block to Irma's house, she was filled with gloomy forebodings. For all she knew, Irma might have a part-time maid who was in possession of the apartment or might arrive while Myra was there. The fact that no one had answered the phone meant nothing. The maid might have arrived after she phoned. And what right had she to assume that the key she held in her damp, nervous hand would open the door to the apartment? Irma had demanded in no uncertain tone that Lester return the key he had confiscated from her desk. Perhaps he *had* returned it on Monday night *after* the last cylinder had dropped into the trough. Then the key she had had copied would be some unknown and unimportant one which was of no earthly use where Irma's door was concerned. Or, granting that it actually was the key to the apartment, it might be, not the key to the street door, but to the lobby door. That meant Myra would have to enter the building itself and run the gantlet of the doorman and the elevator boy. She could not under any circumstances afford to do that. Finally, it could be the key to the street door but in these days of slipshod workmanship, the key might need some filing and adjusting before it would fit and open the door. Too late, she felt she should have kept Lester's key and slipped the duplicate on his key ring.

She reached the house. There was plenty of traffic in the street but few pedestrians. She rang the street doorbell twice. Nobody came. With fast-beating heart, hiding her action with her body, she tried the key in the lock. The Amsterdam Avenue German was a good workman. With silent ease, the key turned, and the door opened. She slipped quickly in and closed the door after her. There was a bolt on the door, and she pushed that on. She did the same to the lobby door and breathed a trifle easier. At least no one could enter and take her unawares.

A narrow hall opening from the street door bisected the little apartment from north to south. On the left was a door, giving onto the living room, a well-proportioned, attractive room, its two windows facing Fifty-Seventh Street. Its far wall separated it from the lobby of the apartment house. Behind the living room was a pretty breakfast nook which, in turn, led to a small kitchen. On the right-hand side of the center hall, another door led to Irma's bedroom which also faced the street. Behind it was a pink-tiled bathroom. The kitchen and bathroom windows opened on an inner court. At the back of the hall, between the bathroom and kitchen, a third door led to a roomy closet. The whole place was dim and cool. Irma kept the Venetian blinds down for the sake of privacy, and the windows were closed, as the apartment was air-conditioned.

Myra walked through the rooms, memorizing every detail. The door which opened into the lobby of the building was in the breakfast nook. She stood for a moment figuring her chances of getting out of one exit if she were trapped by someone coming in the other door. The chances were poor. The breakfast nook could only be reached through the living room. However, if someone entered from the lobby, she could possibly escape from the hall or bedroom through the street door without detection. As far as cover went, the large closet at the back of the hall seemed the best bet.

Without removing her thin summer gloves, she first inspected the bathroom medicine cabinet. There was a scanty array of bottles, one of aspirin, another of Castile hair shampoo, and suchlike harmless items. A jar of cleansing cream and a box of bath salts comprised the cosmetics. Irma's invincible beauty required little assistance from art. As Myra remembered, the only make-up the girl had ever used was lipstick and that very sparingly. Of the poison, formerly a part of Neves, D.D.S.'s equipment, there was absolutely no trace.

Still with gloves on, Myra went through the Empire desk in the living room. The gun was not there. She riffled through the papers in the drawers and pigeonholes. There were bills, invitations, laundry lists, and one innocent but amusing item— a notebook headed *Horses that owe me money*, followed by a number of names such as Devil Dog, Flying Centaur, and so on. With a grin, Myra deduced that the canny Irma would continue to bet on those horses until they finally won and returned her investment in them. The desk yielded nothing else. With a purposeful air, Myra abstracted an old laundry list in Irma's writing and three sheets of her monogrammed notepaper, dropping them into her bag.

She began a systematic search for the gun, tackling the bedroom first. She opened every drawer of the bureau, vanity table, and lowboy. She found nothing. She slipped her hand under the bedcovers in a sweeping motion between the mattress and the box spring. There was no gun.

Suddenly a bell shrilled through the apartment. She stood, paralyzed, her heartbeats suffocating her. When she could move, she tiptoed to the hall, to see if she could discern the shadow of a figure on the opaque glass panels of the street door. The glass was clear. Then it was the lobby doorbell which had rung. She could let herself out onto the street with safety, if she went now. But some stubborn, indomitable instinct in her refused to turn tail. If she fled now, before finding the gun, who knew when she would find another opportunity with a clear coast? If she did not accomplish her purpose today, her time schedule would be shot to pieces, her whole plan disorganized, and her fight to beat Irma and Lester at their own game lost. This was a duel to the death, and she refused to give ground. She stood waiting for a second ring. It did not come. After a full five minutes, she crept to the breakfast nook. Under the lobby door, something white glimmered on the floor. It had not been there earlier, and she realized, with exquisite relief, that the hall man had undoubtedly given a perfunctory ring and then slipped a letter under the door. She stooped and saw that it was an ad from a fur storage company. Ruefully, she told herself that these worthies had unwittingly shortened her life by at least a year.

She went back to the bedroom. Only the clothes closet was left. Climbing on a chair, she investigated the shelves first. Her earlier forebodings had vanished. The fact that the key had worked and the knowledge that she had not let herself be scared away, combined to give her back her belief in her own star. She would not consider the possibility that Irma had returned the gun to Steve. The gun was here, and she would find it.

The shelves were piled with boxes, some huge, and carefully marked *Manhasset winter coats, suits, and dresses*. Myra did not even undo their heavy cords. Irma was burning no bridges until she reached the far shore of wealth—wealth of any kind, whether Myra's or some unfortunate, beguiled lover's. Until then, the Manhasset clothing was a backlog, too useful to throw out. There was a box containing a magnificent new alligator handbag, with Harlan James's card still in it, and addressed to *My Moonlight Madonna*. Myra bit a cynical lip and searched on. In an old cigar box, she came upon the trophies salvaged from the unfortunate Dr. Neves's medicine cabinet. There was a small round box marked plainly *Arsenic,* another of strychnine, a tiny heavy container of mercury, and a few less dangerous items such as powdered pumice, a roll of dental rubber, and a small bottle of Campho-Phenique. She stood, considering deeply. She wanted with every fiber in her, to dump the poisons down the drain. But she did not dare. If Irma looked for them and found them gone, all her suspicions would be roused. If she did not look for them, then they were no menace, lying on the shelf. She did decide, however, that if she found no gun, she would take away a quantity of the strychnine as a substitute. It would pose a problem to work it into her scheme, but it had the advantage that it was traceable to Irma.

Immediately afterward, she found the little automatic in an empty Sherry candy box. It was loaded, as Steve had said.

Another problem faced her. She had to take the gun, but she ran the risk that between this afternoon and tomorrow night, Irma might do what she had threatened—insist on Steve's taking the gun back. If she did and found it missing, it complicated things again, for Myra. But this was a risk she had to take. And in her optimistic frame of mind, she felt that there was no great danger. If Irma had intended returning the gun, would she have put it high up on a shelf in her closet? Myra thought not.

Carefully, she rearranged every box on the shelf exactly as she had found it. She descended from the chair, dusted off the seat to remove any marks from her feet, and put it back in its place. She wrapped the gun in a handkerchief and dropped it in her bag. She unbolted the lobby door and then let herself out of the street door.

Twenty minutes later, she submitted herself to the expert ministrations of Francine.

This was Wednesday, July second.

CHAPTER XIX

When Lester came into Myra's room on Thursday morning, even he could not simulate admiration for a fresh morning look on her face. She looked utterly done in. Her eyes were heavy and red-rimmed, with purplish stains beneath them. Her skin, sallower than usual, justified his phrase "little yellow cheek." A second sleepless night had robbed her of any semblance of even young middle age. She looked ravaged. It was not fear alone which had kept her awake this second night. A revulsion of bitter humiliation and hate had swept over her again. Dry-eyed and writhing, she had stared into the dark, hearing again the shocking dialogue on the cylinders. She pictured them standing in the study, insolent in their young bloom, uttering their cold-blooded words, planning callously to kill her for her cash. There was something horrifying about their composure, their lack of emotion as they weighed the disadvantages of the various methods of slaughter. The only animation they had displayed had been when they hit upon the idea of accidental death for her. That roused them; it would save their skins. She felt that if she had tried to delineate evil in a play, she would not have dared to draw characters so ruthless; her audience would not have believed her.

In the night watches, she compared herself to them. She was planning to be just as ruthless as they, but was she, too, essentially vile? She honestly believed she was not. She cited the many young people she had assisted, her devotion to her work which gave pleasure to thousands. An utterly selfish person of her means would have wasted her life in the pursuit of mere pleasure, instead of the grueling travail of writing.

She gave full value to the dreadfulness of what she was doing. But there were extenuating circumstances. These two, deceptive in their astounding beauty, were worse than worthless. They were a real menace to the world, he a pimp preying on others, a bloodsucker and a jackal; she an all-but-acknowledged murderess, a Borgia with a sadistic hatred of human life. They were, truly, better dead.

Beside the moral aspect, there was the question of her own safety. Self-preservation was the inalienable right of every human being. Call it murder, but to her storm-tossed mind, it was justified murder.

Lester removed her breakfast tray and tipped up her chin with loving concern.

"Darling, I ought to be shot. We shouldn't have stayed out so late last night. It was too much for you."

Myra, alert now, and completely set in her chosen path, used the opening instantly.

"It wasn't that, Les. I'll have to confess. It's my work again."

"Damn your work, then!"

"I know. I almost feel the same."

"You'll tear yourself to pieces."

"I've struck another snag. I was awake half the night fighting it."

"I won't have it, darling! You mustn't!"

"And it's such a tiny point, too."

"I don't care what it is—"

"I wonder—if you could help me—"

"*I?* Help *you?*"

"What's so odd about that?"

"A dub like me?"

"Stop underestimating yourself, Les dear. Of course you don't know the mechanics of writing. How should you? But you've got judgment—and what I need like bread just now—a good sound *masculine* point of view."

"Darling! If I only could! To be of some real use to you!"

"You're sweet. And even if you can't suggest anything, it might help me to talk it out. Sometimes ideas just spark out of the air."

"Try me, honey."

"Well, here's the situation. This chap—he's a college professor, but young—is happily married. One of his coeds—the free-love, uninhibited species—goes for him in a big way, and makes no bones about telling him. His wife's the jealous type, and he's in mortal fear she'll spot this kid's yen for him and raise a row. He's got to choke the kid off somehow. Now how's he going to tell her he wants no part of her?"

"I suppose—plain words would be best."

"I've tried that—cylinder after cylinder of it. He sounds like a self-righteous prig. It's a ticklish spot. He is, after all, the hero."

"I see. Well—" He stopped, at a loss.

"I thought perhaps you—the man's angle— Put yourself in his place. How would you tell her?"

He swelled visibly.

"I'd still use plain words," he pronounced.

"That tells me nothing. *Use* them. I need a few crisp telling phrases that dish out the truth to the kid but don't make him an unmitigated heel."

Lester was a quick study. He had absorbed her phrases and now brought them out promptly, quite convinced that they were his own.

"Well, I'd simply say, 'My dear girl, if you can be uninhibited, so can I. You say you love me and make no bones about it. Can you take it as well as dish it? Well, I *don't* love you. If you think me a heel, get this—it happens. I'm in love with my wife.'" He looked at her uncertainly. "Lousy, eh?"

Myra leaned toward him in undisguised admiration.

"Les, that's marvelous! Clark Gable stuff to the life! Quick, say it again and don't change a word."

He repeated it practically verbatim.

"'My dear girl,'" she echoed after him. "'If you can be uninhibited, so can I'—or— You'd better jot it down for me, Les. I want it exactly the way you said it. There's a pad on the desk." If Lester noticed that the pad was his own, he made no comment. As gratified as a Gold Star child in 1A, he wrote down the speech painstakingly. As he tossed the pad on the bed, she added, "You've just about saved me, darling."

"It was nothing," he said modestly.

"If you only knew how you've helped me!" She regarded him through half-closed eyes. "Y'know, dear, I think you're photogenic. You'd screen well."

His face lit up.

"Myra! Honey! You mean— It's the kind of part I'd adore—"

She shook her head regretfully.

"If only you could act," she murmured.

A red tide swept his face. He turned away to hide the frustrated resentment in his eyes.

He got out of the room as soon as he decently could. Instantly Myra scrambled out of bed and, holding the pad carefully by the edges, wrapped it in a scarf and placed it in the drawer with the gun, Irma's notepaper and laundry list, the wig and grease paint, and, lastly, the key. Her set of props was complete.

In her bath, she chuckled maliciously.

"If that wasn't the carrot and the donkey, then I'm a pulp writer. He's just about frothing. That's all to the good. The madder he is, the more intent he'll be on his own pretty plans and the less he'll notice what I'm about." Her mouth curved bitterly. "It's the first time the mask has slipped. I wonder he didn't strangle me there and then. But no—not my cagey Lester. *He* wants to eat his cake and own the whole bakeshop." The iron of his treachery had seared so deeply, her heart felt as callous as a rhinoceros hide.

Ten minutes later, carrying several of her props wrapped in the scarf, she locked herself in the study. But her activities were not her usual ones. There was no pacing up and down, no dictating, no original creation. The work today was purely imitative.

She drew on a pair of thin loose gloves which did not hamper her at all. She exposed the pad with Lester's written words on it and copied his little "speech" over and over again, until she mastered the essentials of his script. She worked for nearly an hour before she felt she was ready.

Detaching a sheet of his paper from the back end of the pad, she began to write, slowly, carefully, with constant glances at his writing. This time, creative effort entered into her task. The finished product was a six-line note, in a credible imitation of Lester's hand.

Next she took out Irma's laundry list and for a long time wrote *Sheets Pillowslips Napkins* over and over again. Irma's bold dark vertical writing was easy to copy. Finally when Myra's list looked enough like Irma's to satisfy her critical eye, she embarked on another short bit of original composition. This time the result, when transcribed in Irma's writing, on Irma's notepaper, consisted of a mere two lines. But, she thought, they were potent. She surveyed her handiwork critically. It would pass, even if Irma and Lester had ever seen a sample of each other's writing, which she doubted. After all, they had known each other a bare month, and so far as she could imagine, had never had a need to write to each other. If either one had, she relied on her very passable imitation, the use of each one's letterhead, and above all, on the exciting contents of the notes to drive suspicion from their minds.

She folded the two notes she had composed until they were about three inches square. Then, still with gloves, she detached Lester's own creation from the pad and crumpled it into a ball, but not so tightly as to destroy the fingerprints which he had so obligingly planted there. She dropped all three notes into the scarf.

The rest of the papers—Irma's laundry list and all her own practice efforts—she burned, disposing of the ashes down the drain.

The scarf, with its precious burden, she took to her room and locked again in her bureau. It was half past one. When she descended to the dining room for lunch, she was relieved that Lester was not present. Austin informed her that Mr. Blaine had left the house at eleven-thirty and would be back around six. He had not said where he was bound for.

Myra digested this silently; Lester was still angry. It was almost the first time he had ever left without a definite message. She reproached herself for carelessness in not sending him again on some errand that would keep him away from Irma during these last crucial hours. Then suddenly, she remembered that Irma had a fitting today. The white satin Schiaparelli became Myra's ally. No doubt, Lester was safely at Green Hollow and Irma's day, before and after her fitting, occupied in buying accessories for the Schiaparelli. Of course, nothing was 100 percent safe. She wasn't exactly God. A few minor details had to be left to chance. But she mustn't fog her mind with doubts and fears.

Eve came into the dining room just after Myra, and they talked absently as they ate. Myra's mind was full of a thousand small tricky details, and Eve was nervously wondering what Mr. and Mrs. Street, Senior, of Southampton were going to think of an undistinguished little private secretary whose tilted nose and wide mouth precluded any claims to beauty.

"I've cleared up all unfinished business," she told Myra. "If there are any cylinders to transcribe, I can do them this afternoon. Miles isn't coming until four."

"He's back from Washington?"

"He got in at twelve."

Myra pondered. Perhaps when Miles came, she ought to have him draw up the new will in simple form today and not postpone it until Monday. But her optimism surged back; she was so certain of the success of her plan that she felt she could afford to wait.

On the other hand, the cylinders demanded immediate consideration. She would have liked to grind them underfoot until they were indistinguishable scraps of wax but some instinct of caution held her back. If her intricate scheme failed in any one point, the whole delicate fabric would collapse. She might very well be in danger of arrest for premeditated murder. Without the cylinders, her case would be the ordinary one of an aging jealous wife killing her erring husband. With the cylinders, the husband and his accomplice would stand convicted of intent to murder her, and her actions could be interpreted as self-defense of a sort. At least, her position would be infinitely improved with the record of that incriminating dialogue at hand.

She thought of hiding them somewhere in the house but came to the sensible conclusion that nowhere would they be as inconspicuous as in their trough in the study. Only Eve was likely to disturb them, and again she safeguarded herself against that danger.

"No cylinders to transcribe. I'm still battling with the scene. I'll play them over and over until I discover what's wrong."

"Perhaps if we both listened to them—" suggested Eve.

"No. Go up and primp for your presentation at court."

"I'd rather be busy. I'm in a blue funk."

"You needn't be. The Streets are homey people. You'll appeal to them just as you are—worse luck for me!"

"It's nothing like as far along as that. Miles just thought it would be nice to spend the Fourth together down there."

"Don't tell me I've been harboring a ninny for three years. Miles has aisles in his eyes."

"I know it. I might have known I couldn't fool you."

"Run along, then. I'm going to be busy. Have a good time."

Rid of Eve, she went to her room and opened a large case containing costume jewelry. There were clips, earrings, bracelets, and necklaces of semiprecious stones, and stones of no intrinsic value except for their workmanship. She selected three necklaces and put them in a smaller jewel box, where they lay awaiting their brief appearance in the night's drama. Next, she took out the box of grease paints she had brought down from the attic. The next half hour she spent in make-up experiments on her left foot. Finally satisfied, she put the box back in the bureau drawer, locked the drawer, and pocketed the key.

She left her room and went down the hall to the guest room Irma had occupied during her visit. It was a delightful room decorated in dull blue and silver. It faced east, and the immense long, low picture window framed a lovely view of the river. The window was so large and heavy that a stout window pole stood beside it such as are used in schoolrooms. She pushed open the window with the pole. It slid up as silently as if it were oiled. She closed it again and looked about the room, checking details with her eyes. She went back to her own room and returned with a pair of long, heavy shears. She put the shears in the drawer of the vanity table and went out, closing the door behind her.

Back in her room, she went over her agenda again. For the moment, she could do no more. She was dead tired. For two nights she had not slept at all. Wisely, she slipped off her dress and lay down. Sleep did not come. The thought of the cylinders nagged at her like a wasp. Her pride and vanity cried aloud to destroy them. The annihilation of Lester and Irma was hardly more important to her than the necessity for saving face. No matter how smoothly her plan went, it would be as dust and ashes to her, if the truth got out. Echoes of comment by the world crossed her tired mind and formed themselves into galling phrases.

"Poor Myra." "What could she expect—cradle snatching a babe in arms like young Blaine?" "They do say that women of a certain age— But I gave Myra credit for more self-control, poor girl." "Poor? If you ask me, it was coming to her. Well, she won't be quite so snooty in future."

It was something she could not face. She would smash the loathsome things the instant it was all over. Well—not the instant, but just as soon as she saw how things were going. A day or two would tell the tale. Then she could be rid of them forever. Until then, her nagging sense of caution told her to keep them in reserve.

She was suddenly, heavily, dreamlessly asleep, and awakened only when Lester came clattering into her room. He kissed her as affectionately as if there had never been the little passage at arms that morning about his talent as an actor.

"Wake up, honey chile. Tonight you'll be Queen of the May," he said gaily.

She was instantly alert. Her eyes sought the black-and-gold electric clock on her mantel. It was ten minutes to six. She stretched lazily and luxuriously without the least appearance of hurry.

"Hello. I must have dozed off for a minute."

"Probably needed it, but good, you work-demon."

"It's late. Alice said to come early."

"Plenty of time."

"How was the golf?" she asked casually.

"No golf. Tony and I were looking at a crop of yearlings up at East View. How would you like to own a stable, baby?"

"My grandfather had the biggest stable in America in his day." So he had not been with Irma. That was all to the good. "Well, run along now, dear. It takes you longer to dress than it does me."

"Them's lyin' words, madam."

She pushed him playfully out of the room.

She waited until she heard him splashing in his shower, singing lustily as usual. Then she ran downstairs and out to the garage where she swiftly unlocked the padlock which fastened the double doors. It was risky; Mrs. Link might see her from the kitchen window, but it was a chance she was forced to take. The garage doors had to be open.

Back in her room, she dialed Irma's number. This was the afternoon of Thursday, July third.

CHAPTER XX

Irma stood before her mirror, eying herself critically. In spite of her beauty, or perhaps because of its unassailable perfection, she had curiously little vanity. She accepted her loveliness as an asset on a par with her bank balance and just as expendable. Tonight it must work for her, weave the web about Steve Thatcher, tighter and more binding. She might have need of him after tonight's dinner at Alice Grier's.

Inwardly she raged at the failure of her efforts on Steve's terrace Tuesday night. The inopportune appearance of the butler Perez, just as she was hustling Myra along to her death over the parapet, was maddening. In her balked fury, she could gladly have killed him as well as Myra.

Time was growing short. Three full days had passed since she and Lester had discovered Myra's treacherous intention of disinheriting him. It had seemed easy, that night, to decide on an innocent-appearing accident. But actually, it was damnably difficult. Sudden death could be dealt out if one were determined enough, but the snag lay in killing Myra without casting a breath of suspicion on either Lester or herself. Anything that would jeopardize his inheritance of the Hudson fortune rendered the murder worse than useless. Lester, in particular, must be in the clear. If she herself were suspected, it would not be so bad, mainly because there seemed no motive for her to desire the death of her benefactor. But if tonight at the Grier dinner, she did succeed in her plans, she, along with the rest of the guests, would come in for a share of suspicion and possibly accusation. Hence, her determination to hold Steve to her with ropes of silk as binding as steel. With Steve Thatcher to defend her, she was 90 percent sure of defeating any charge of murder. For the other 10 percent, she relied on the effect of her beauty on any jury.

She hated the necessity for using poison after all, but she had no choice. Tonight was possibly the last evening they would all be together before Monday. She grinned a little as she remembered telling Lester on the phone this morning that her plans were not yet perfected. She did not dare tell him that when she administered the arsenic to Myra, she intended slipping a smaller harmless dose to Lester himself. It was the only way she could think of to keep suspicion from him. It had, too, another good purpose. If both Myra and Lester—and nobody else—showed the symptoms of poisoning, it would point to something they ate or drank *before* coming to the Griers', doing much to clear Alice's guests of guilt.

She looked ravishing. The shining white Schiaparelli satin fell in suave folds to her feet, following the perfect lines of her body. Her creamy shoulders and slim column of throat rose above it, innocent of jewelry. The thick gold waves of her hair rippled back from her face, framing its purity of contour and color. Her appraising glance commended what it saw, but somewhat absently. Her mind was busy with a problem, how carry the arsenic to Alice Grier's and how get rid of all traces of it afterward? It was very possible that they might all be searched on the spot. She finally decided on wrapping it in a Kleenex, innocent-looking in her evening bag and easily disposable afterward.

She had just finished tucking the small lethal parcel in her bag when the lobby doorbell rang. She gave herself one last fleeting glance in the mirror.

"Now do your stuff. Hand him the old charm till he's yours to command."

She took a deep breath and opened the door. Steve stood there, a small florist's box in his hand.

"Hello," Irma smiled. "You're nice and early."

"The longer to look at you, my dear."

"So now you *admit* you're a wolf." She laughed.

"I'm a besotted swine before Circe. Anything so breathtakingly lovely—" He threw the florist's box on a table. "Those are orchids, rare and beautiful. Stick 'em in the garbage pail. The flower isn't grown that could improve your looks."

"I'm glad you think so. You are certainly a good judge."

"I'm limp, like a kid at its first Christmas tree. I could do with a drink to get my bearings again."

"That's the ultimate compliment, Steve. Liquor to make you sober after *my* effect on you."

"Irma—my lovely—you're so approachable tonight—"

"Approachable! Steve, you utter fool, I'm so defenseless, so susceptible—I wonder, are you really as clever as they say?"

She gritted her teeth and bore the violent kiss he ground upon her mouth. By main force, she steeled herself against wrenching away from him. She loathed being touched. She did finally manage to extricate herself.

"You've just about wrecked my make-up," she scolded. "Go help yourself to a drink while I repair the damage. Although—perhaps you'd better not. There'll be drinks going at Myra's."

"Myra's?"

"Yes. We're stopping by for her."

"Damn! I don't even have you to myself from here to Eleventh Street."

"She particularly phoned and asked me."

"A royal command."

"Well, yes," she returned seriously. "Nothing's too much for me to do for Myra."

"I know, I know," he retorted impatiently. "She saved your life."

"More than that," she said with a candid gaze straight into his eyes. "If it hadn't been for her, I'd never have met you." With an impish grin which took the curse of banality from her words, she ducked into her bedroom.

A few minutes later she returned, carrying her silver lamé evening wrap and bag. He took them both from her and laid his hands on her shoulders. She could smell the liquor on his breath. That, combined with the annoying touch of his hands, nearly broke her self-control. She had always had a quick, ungovernable temper, and it took all her will power not to flare into fury. Instead, she said as lightly as she could, "No, Steve, not again! My supply of lipstick is limited."

With a shrug, he slipped her wrap about her and handed her the evening bag.

Together, they left the apartment by the street door. Steve's long, shining Lincoln stood at the curb, his trim chauffeur standing at attention beside it. They got in and drove the single block to Myra's.

CHAPTER XXI

Looking like a Greek god in modern dress, Lester came into Myra's room, just as she herself was ready. For a warm summer night, her costume was rather odd. She wore a *robe de style* of white, with a tight bodice and a long full skirt. Her shoulders were bare and only the tips of her small high-heeled slippers showed beneath the billowing folds. The effect was distinctly formal and practically demanded the addition of the sixteen-button gloves she was drawing on as Lester entered.

He looked her over with his customary appreciative eye and said, "Darling, you look wonderful. But, gosh, honey, you could be going to a cotillion. Isn't it a teeny bit flossy for just a bridge game?" He opened the big crystal cigarette box on the table and filled his gold cigarette case from it.

"You're absolutely right, Les. But it just came home and I couldn't resist it." She did not add that she had to wear a dress with which gloves would not appear out of place. "Shall I change?"

"Of course not. Give 'em an eyeful. You'll knock 'em dead."

"With Irma around? I won't have a look-in."

"That's what *you* think. Irma's gorgeous but she hasn't got your distinction. She's just something off a candy box."

"What a comfort you are, honey! Look, Les, a cocktail would be nice when they get here."

"They?"

"Irma and Steve. They're calling for us."

"How come?"

"Well, after all, why not? But the main reason is, I've got something for Irma."

"You always have. I think you'd give her your shirt if it fit her."

"Silly! Run along and mix the Martinis. Yours are so much better than Austin's. I'll be down in a minute."

Alone, Myra lifted the edge of her skirt and surveyed her left foot searchingly. Satisfied with what she saw, she dropped the flowing folds with a smile. She unlocked her bureau drawer and took out a long white silk scarf, plain except for a six-inch band of heavy silver brocade across each end. By snipping a few of the stitches attaching the brocade to the silk, she had achieved a small pocket in one end of the scarf. Into this pocket, she slipped the two folded notes she had so laboriously written that morning. She threw the scarf about her shoulders, fastened it in front with a quaint dull-silver pin, and relocked the bureau drawer. She was ready for action.

But instead of following Lester downstairs, she waited, quiescent, for the rise of the curtain on the evening's drama. The ringing of the bell was the prompter's cue. Without haste she moved to the top of the stairs just as Austin admitted Irma and Steve into the wide entrance hall below. Lester, a frosted shaker in his hands, appeared from the dining room.

Myra waited until the babble of their greetings subsided. Then she called down lightly, "Hello, you people!"

They all looked up with a word or a wave. Lester said, "Come down, honey. The Martinis are hot off the griddle."

"Lower the light, then," she tossed back. "I want Irma up here for a minute."

Irma was standing at the console mirror, smoothing the

slightly ruffled waves of her hair. Even in the one block to Myra's, Steve had tried to follow up his earlier advantage. Irma's bag lay on the console table beside her. Lester stood directly behind her, the shaker still in his hands.

"Make it snappy, Irma," he said. "You'll pass in a crowd. And these cocktails really won't wait."

Irma ignored him and raised her head to Myra.

"Be right with you," she called.

Suddenly Myra caught her breath. Irma had turned to come up the stairs but she was leaving her bag on the table. It was all Myra could do to choke back a scream of rage. Such a trifle, such a tiny unforeseen slip, and it meant the wreck of all her plans. In that instant, she was so utterly furious at Irma, she could have killed her with her bare hands. And then Irma turned, caught up the bag, and started up the stairs. By the time she reached the top, Myra had her voice once more under control. She hooked her arm in Irma's and steered her toward the bedroom with a continuous breezy flow of talk.

"Fool that I was, Irma! After you *told* me you were wearing white! I should have shunned it like the plague. You're staggering, child. There ought to be a frame around you, with indirect picture lighting. Also, there ought to be a law against you. You're pure poison to all women for miles around." She gave Irma a critical sidewise look. "I was right, though. A necklace *will* take away that look of 'too too solid flesh.'"

"I would have worn something of my own," Irma replied, ignoring the whimsy and going to the point that interested her. "But when you said you had a necklace for me, there was no sense putting one on, just to take it off here."

They had reached Myra's room. Skillfully, naturally, Myra managed to ease off Irma's wrap and guide it, as well as her bag, to a careless heap on the bed.

"On the bureau," said Myra. "In the oblong box. There are three of them. Take your pick."

With alacrity, Irma advanced to the bureau, while Myra, for a fraction of time, busied herself beneath the folds of the wrap on the bed, keeping up her inconsequential chatter. It was a matter of seconds and one of the notes found its way from

Myra's scarf to the large flat compact in Irma's bag,

"The opals, of course, are the most valuable, if you're not superstitious. The topazes go beautifully with your hair. And the lapis lazuli brings out all the creamy tints of your skin."

Now Myra was beside her at the bureau, with an effect of having been right at her heels all the time.

"Say what you will, there's nobody like Schiaparelli, is there? But of course, you could wear a flour sack and give it an air."

The canny Irma chose the valuable opals.

"I love these," she said. "Thanks ever so." For the first time she gave a real look at Myra and added, "White's a *good* color for you. It makes you look so—alive."

Myra dropped her exultant eyes. This girl was shrewd. Together, they walked to the top of the stairs. There Myra stopped.

"Oh, my wrap!" she exclaimed and darted back to the bedroom while Irma went on down the stairs. A minute later, Myra reappeared, a silver wrap over her arm. Lester and Steve stood at the console table, watching Austin pour out the cocktails. Irma was on her way to join them.

Lester was saying, "You're sure you chilled the glasses, Austin?"

Myra's moment was at hand. About four steps from the bottom, she made a sharp noise with her heel, snatched at the banister, and, with a scream, landed in a heap on the floor.

All four rushed toward her, where she lay, her wide skirt about her, like a dancer making a deep curtsey.

"Darling! Myra!" Lester's voice rose anxiously.

She waited a brief second, her eyes closed, her face distorted with pain. Then she gasped, "It's nothing—I tripped over my wrap—just give me a minute—"

They waited.

"Now—Les, if you'll give me a hand—"

He kicked the skirt aside and stooped, his arm around her waist. He got her upright.

"I'll see if I can stand on it—"

She made the attempt and collapsed with a moan on the bottom step. They were all, even Austin, standing in a semicircle before her.

She sat there, a brave little woman with the determined smile of courage on her lips belying the suffering in her eyes. Inwardly, she was thinking furiously.

How soon would the damned thing turn color if it were real? Would any of them know? Steve might. Well, she couldn't sit here all night. She'd have to risk it.

Slowly she leaned over and turned up the hem of the white skirt. Her small brocaded slipper came into view, and above it, distinct under the sheer stocking, an angry pink-and-lilac blotch over her ankle.

Lester gave a sympathetic cry, Steve a whistle of indrawn breath. Myra dropped the skirt. They had seen. That was all she wanted. She couldn't stand a microscope trained on it—or even a close look. She raised whimsical eyes, the brave painful smile still pasted on her lips.

"There goes the ball game. Les, get me upstairs and phone Alice quickly. She can always get one more for bridge."

"*One* more?"

"Yes."

"I'm not going, either. I'll put you to bed and get the doctor."

He scooped her gently into his arms, the white skirt billowing like a cloud.

"Don't be silly, Les, dear. It's sweet of you but it's totally unnecessary. A good soak in hot water—"

"You heard me, darling. Alice can dig up two players."

They continued the argument all the way up the stairs and into her room. Under cover of it, Myra's hands were frantically busy. When Les laid her gently on her bed, her heart was beating with triumph. The second note was in his cigarette case.

"Now, toss me a nightgown, go phone Alice—I *wish* you'd do me a favor and go without me—and tell Austin to fill an ice bag. On a summer night, it's better than a hot bath and just as effective."

She threw everything she had of energy and persuasiveness into her tone. Lester, driven by the force of her stronger personality, as usual, went about the various errands.

Alone, she tore out of her clothes and into bed. When Irma

came up to be of service, the first dangerous moments were over. Irma was rigid with frustration. Another chance gone. But perhaps something could be salvaged. If she and Lester were here tonight alone, with Myra helpless

She said sympathetically, "Alice will understand if I duck it, too, and stay. I'm good with a bandage."

"You'll all make me ill with your hysterics. You'd think I'd fractured my skull." Les, followed by Steve, appeared at the door. "Now get this, all of you," she went on with just the right mixture of pluck and exasperation. "I've sprained my ankle, and it hurts like the devil. I can't stand on it. So what? I'll use an ice bag and if it isn't better in the morning, I'll have Edgar take a look. I've a swell book for company, so for God's sake, stop treating me like something made of sugar and go on to Alice's before her dinner's ruined."

Steve agreed and overbore all of Irma's objections.

They did finally go, all but Lester. He was firm in his determination to stand by and smooth the bed of sickness.

As the two others went downstairs, Steve said to Irma, "That's a remarkable relationship. By all the laws of nature that boy ought to be philandering nineteen to the dozen. And Myra ought to be reaping a crop of very sorry wild oats. Whereas—"

"Oh, yes," Irma agreed. "They really are an ideal couple." Inwardly, she was seething with rage.

Upstairs, Myra was turning over this new fact of Lester's presence in the house. In one way, it was perfect. Her two notes were now planted. It was practically certain that they would both be read long before midnight. Irma would undoubtedly use her compact when she arrived at the Griers'. And Lester would smoke a cigarette, whether he was at home or out. With Lester here, there was no chance of a whispered word between the two, which might have been catastrophic. Myra's whole plan was a terrific gamble, and it was a relief to obviate one element of risk.

But with Lester here, her method of procedure around midnight took on an added trickiness. She would have to plan nearly to the split second and she would have to watch Lester's movements with the eye of a hawk. For a moment, she quailed before the hair-trigger delicacy upon which everything hinged. But as she thought again of that recorded dialogue on the cylinders, her whole body tensed with the determination to go on, if it destroyed her—as it very well could.

CHAPTER XXII

Austin knocked and came in with the ice bag wrapped in a towel. Lester hurried to take it and approached the bed to adjust it to her foot.

"Better let me," she said, reaching for it. "Oh—Austin—"

"Yes, madame?"

"Sorry to trouble you, but you'll have to scare up some sort of scratch meal for Mr. Blaine and me."

"Certainly, madame. Of course, I can't go so far as a roast with Mrs. Link gone, but there is some jellied salmon, and quite a good cut of Stilton and I believe I could turn out acceptable coffee if you will permit."

Myra smiled.

"It sounds ravishing, Austin. I hope it doesn't interfere with your evening."

"Not at all, madame. I had no intention of going out. These air-cooled cinemas invariably induce a cold, I find."

Myra stifled a chuckle. Austin was the epitome of all the English butlers of stage, screen, and story. He was an imposing figure, dignified and fiftyish. But his life held a dark secret; he had been born on Tenth Avenue. For years, he had fooled all his employers, but he never felt quite at ease with Myra. There was a quizzical look in her eyes at times which made him feel that she had bored through his rich British accent to the gashouse twang beneath. He thought her much too smart for a woman and disapproved of her highly, but he had a sneaking strong respect for her. He could well understand Lester's devotion to her. Ability and domination had been the standard of excellence in his youthful gang world, and Myra was a born leader, just as Lester was a born follower. For Lester, he had a tolerant, rather insulting, liking.

SUDDEN FEAR

He brought up a tempting-looking serving cart and to Myra's relief, served their portions across the room and placed them on separate trays. She watched Lester sharply. It would be ironic if he managed to administer Irma's poison now, when everything was in train and success in sight. But Lester's behavior was exemplary. He made no suspicious move whatsoever.

While she drank her coffee—served in individual pots, to her satisfaction—she reached for a cigarette from her bed table. Instead of offering the pack to Lester, she negligently dropped it on the bed out of his reach. The device had the hoped-for result. Mechanically, Lester's hand went to his pocket and brought out his gold cigarette case. Through half-closed eyes, Myra watched, holding her breath. With a faint frown of puzzlement, he discovered the bit of folded paper. For one horrible moment, she thought he was going to crumple it and throw it away. But even as he looked, it unfolded far enough to reveal penciled writing inside. His frown deepened to interest. He cast a swift glance at Myra who was innocently blowing a smoke ring. Quickly he palmed the note and took a cigarette. He made a great play of patting all his pockets for a match, then rose and crossed the room to the table with the crystal cigarette box and lighter on it. He stood there for a long moment, his back to Myra.

Her memory reconstructed the lines he was reading, lines written on Irma's notepaper and ostensibly in Irma's hand.

Les, darling, I thought I could stand it but I can't. I want you tonight. I'll ditch Steve at the door. Use your key but don't come before twelve.

The moment passed. His cigarette alight, he returned to her bedside. His fine nostrils flared, his eyes were electric.

At about the same time, two things occurred at widely separated parts of the city. On Seventh Avenue and One Hundred and Thirty-Fifth Street, a slim pretty tawny girl and a dapper seal-brown man were talking.

"But Lily, Miss Eve your friend. And gone away till Monday. What for you hesi-ma-tate?"

"It ain't right, that's what, Alvin Jones."

"She wouldn't mind. I wouldn't hurt it none. Ain't I the best driver in Harlem?"

"I know, but if we was caught, I'd lose my job."

"Who would catch us? Din you tole me the whole family's out for the evening? I'll even fill in what gas I burn up. It's safe as a bet on Joe Louis."

"I don't like it, Alvin."

"Aw, Lily. A holiday eve and all. Betcha if Miss Eve knowed, she'd *ask* you to use her little ole car. Come on, Lily."

"Well—"

Six miles away, in the powder room of Alice Grier's house on Eleventh Street, Irma was again repairing the damages wrought by Steve on the ride down from Myra's. Alice was phoning for a pinch-hitting couple to take the Blaines' places. Irma was alone. As she snapped open her compact, a folded paper fell out. She opened it and read—on Lester's paper and seemingly in his writing:

Darling: I've got it. Tonight or never. And absolutely foolproof. A thousand times better than your poison. Now, get this. Be in our garage exactly at midnight and wait till I come. I'll explain everything. Remember, exactly at midnight. If I don't show up by one o'clock, go home. Destroy this. Darling, I love you.

At nine o'clock, Myra asked Lester, "How would you like to read aloud to me?"

"Love it! What shall it be?"

She knew the actor in him liked to show his prowess. He would enjoy declaiming the lines of a play or even a novel with dialogue. With deliberate malice, she said, "There's an article on the Minimum Basic Agreement in the Author's League Bulletin which I really ought to read."

"But, sweet, it's so dull! It'll send you to sleep."

"That's the whole idea. In fact, I'll take a couple of tablets to help it along." She reached for the box on her bed table, but she did not miss the flash in his eyes, as he recognized the advantage of having her in a drugged sleep around midnight. "The Bulletin's on the desk. And I hope you won't be too bored."

When he returned to the bed with the slim magazine, she was setting down the half-empty glass of water. But the two sleeping tablets were under her pillow. He sat down, found the article, and began to read aloud.

She hardly heard a word. Now was the time to survey the field, plan her exact procedure, check her time schedule, and consider all possible contingencies. Strangely enough, she felt no fear of Lester, although they were practically alone in the house. That very fact constituted her protection. He would never lay himself open to the immediate guilt which would attach to him, if she died under the present circumstances.

Except for Lester, the household was no problem. Eve was gone. For once Myra blessed Miles for his interest in her secretary. Mrs. Link, the cook, had her own home where she supervised her two teenaged daughters after the Blaine dinner hour was over. Tonight, due to the fact that Myra and Lester had expected to dine out, Mrs. Link was already out of the house, as Austin had reported, and would not return until the next morning. Lily, the second maid also "slept out," as the phrase is. Myra, with her writer's curiosity, had often speculated as to how the girl spent her own time. She did not dream that the girl, unknowingly, would constitute a thread in the fabric of tonight's tapestry. Austin was at home, but his room and bath adjoined the kitchen at the back of the house. And Austin was an early retirer and a sound sleeper, as she knew from the past. She had often raided the icebox to the tune of his unbroken snores. A silent exit through the front door would never disturb him.

Lester was the problem. In the alleged note from Irma, he was to be at her apartment no earlier than twelve. That meant that he should leave the house some time between a quarter and five minutes to twelve. Therefore, she herself must leave the house earlier than that, in order to be in the apartment before he arrived. It was here that she could strike the snag which might wreck everything. If she left the house before Lester, what assurance had she that he would not peep into her bedroom before he left, and discover that she was not in her bed? All his suspicion and caution would be roused. He would smell a rat, and the whole setup would collapse.

If she left the house after Lester and used her key to get into Irma's apartment, even the few seconds while she closed the street door and got the gun out of her bag were enough to put him on guard. She was no match for his strength at any time, and the sight of her at Irma's on the night of his first tryst, would rouse his instant savagery. He would kill her or knock her out before she could act.

She decided that leaving the house before him was the lesser of the risks. Perhaps, in his excitement to be gone, he would not even look into her bedroom. Even if he did, she could rig up something to lull his doubts. After all, he would not come into the room, and it would be dark. As far as Lester was concerned, it was much safer to leave before him and arrive at Irma's well before twelve.

Here another tricky element arose. Irma was due at the garage promptly at twelve. If she had read her note, as Myra must assume, she would see to it that the bridge game at the Griers' broke up in plenty of time for her to follow the directions in the note. Steve would bring her home and she would make it her business to get rid of him promptly. That meant that sometime between, say, 11:30 and ten minutes to twelve, Irma would be at the apartment. To be safely ensconced in her hiding place in Irma's hall closet, it was imperative for Myra to be at the apartment before 11:30, well before either Lester or Irma appeared.

She looked at the clock as Lester's voice droned sullenly on. It was 10:25. She noticed that he kept glancing up at her, impatience and eagerness in his swift look. She let her eyes droop sleepily, alternating this with an occasional start as if she had roused from a doze. At long last, she let herself breathe deeply and regularly, as if in a heavy, sound sleep.

After a few minutes, the reading stopped. She heard his chair creak as he leaned toward the bed. She felt his eyes searching her face. She never missed a breath. Then his voice came, soft as a breeze.

"Darling, are you asleep?" He waited and repeated more loudly, "Are you asleep?"

Almost, she laughed aloud; he was convinced she could not hear him, so why waste an extra "darling" on a sleeping, unattractive wife?

Carefully, he got out of the chair, crossed the room, and switched off the lights. As he stood in the open doorway, she could see him through her lashes, outlined against the faint light from the hall. He stood there for interminable minutes watching her. She was ready to scream, but the even, audible rhythm of her breathing never varied.

Finally he closed the door noiselessly and was gone.

CHAPTER XXIII

Now it was Myra who waited. She heard his door across the hall close softly, but she dared take no chances. If he came back at all, it would be within the first few minutes or just as he left the house.

After ten minutes which seemed like an hour, she slipped out of bed. The first thing she did was to wipe her ankle clean of the grease paint. Then she dressed again in the white dress she had worn earlier, and adjusted the yellow wig she had brought down from the attic. In the dark room, with only the reflection of the street lamp for illumination, the white dress, the silver wrap, and the shoulder-long blond hair made a passable imitation of Irma. The outfit served two purposes. The wig made Myra almost unrecognizable at first glance. And while nobody could mistake her for Irma in a decent light or at close quarters, at the moment when she unlocked Irma's street door, a casual passerby or even the doorman of the building, at a distance of thirty feet or so, would get an impression of a blonde in a white dress and a silver wrap opening the door. It might all be theatrical and unnecessary, but then again, it might have its uses.

Next she rolled her counterpane into the semblance of a human body and laid it lengthwise in the bed under her sheet.

For a while, she was stymied in finding something suitable for a head. Finally, she snatched a brown beret from the closet and molded it as well as she could against the pillow to look like her own short grizzled hair. She tiptoed over to the door to get the effect. To an unsuspicious eye, it could just about pass for a sleeping woman.

She pulled on her long gloves, unlocked the bureau drawer, and took out the gun and the crumpled paper containing Lester's written "speech" of that morning. She put them carefully into her bag, trusting that they both retained whatever fingerprints were on them. Irma's key she kept in her glove, handy for instant use. She was ready.

She looked at the clock and was surprised to see how the time had slipped by. It was 11:20. She had no more time to lose. Again she tiptoed to the door. She laid her hand on the knob and with infinite care, began to turn it. Lester's room was across from hers and about four feet down the hall. Luckily, hers was nearer the staircase so that she would not have to pass his on her way. Slowly, noiselessly, she got the knob turned and drew back the door until a narrow line of dim light from the hall came through. It was a space that could have only been measured in millimeters but it was enough to shock her to stone. Lester was in the hall, letting himself cautiously out of his room. Somehow she got her door closed before he turned, and she stood, paralyzed, behind it. Her heart was beating so violently, she could not hear his progress down the hall. She shrank back against the wall, confused, unable to think with the blood pounding in her head. And then she froze altogether. She heard the infinitesimal click as his hand closed on the knob of her door. The door began to move, slowly and silently toward her. She felt herself utterly lost. He could not fail to hear the wild throbbing of her heart, or the short shallow gasps of her breath. She could not see him, the door was between them. He stood, motionless, the door ajar, until she thought she must tear the air with scream after scream.

Then, just as silently, the door closed again, the knob was released with only that faint, telltale click, and he was gone. She put her ear to the panel and caught the faint sound of his feet on the broad, uncarpeted oak stairs. When he reached the bottom, she dared to open her door carefully and heard him let himself out the front door.

She flew to her window to see which way he went. He had turned right—the way to Irma's. As she watched him, an overpowering rage against him swept over her. The fool, the overeager, greedy imbecile! He would reach Irma's too soon and Steve would see him—*Irma* would see him! All her careful planning would be smashed. They would put their heads together and disavow the writing of the two notes. They would piece the sorry, stagey plot together and know that only she could have concocted it. They would be on their guard and masters of the situation. They would realize that she knew too much and had to be silenced at once. What better time than tonight when they believed her to be tied to her bed with a sprained ankle? Or would they believe that now? Would they return here together—stealthily—ruthlessly—

Suddenly she stiffened. Lester had reached the corner. Under the street light, he lifted his arm and looked at his wristwatch. Then he veered and went into the shabby bar that stood on the corner.

Like a reprieved prisoner, she snatched her bag, dashed out of her room, down the stairs, and out of the door. Looking neither right or left, she hurried along the street, all caution thrown to the winds. Before her excitement died down, she had reached Irma's door, used her key, and found herself in the dark narrow hall, the door safely closed behind her. She leaned against it, panting, weak in every nerve and muscle of her body. There was a buzzing in her head and dizzy circles of light swirled before her in the darkness.

She ground her teeth together. She must not faint. She would beat them yet. Everything was all right. Lester was safely in the bar. Of course he realized he must not show near Irma's while there was a chance that Steve could see him. She might have known. Where his own hide was concerned, Lester was shrewd enough. If, later, a fatality happened to Myra, a man of Steve's brains would wonder. Lester was too cagey to give him food for suspicion. He would be careful to arrive well after twelve. Her breath became more regular, her mind began to function again.

But Irma was due any minute. Myra must not be found here. Carefully, she felt her way down the dark little hall and opened the closet door at the back. It was good-sized and nearly empty. As she recalled, only a raincoat and a bulky paper moth bag hung in it. She turned the bag as nearly broadside as she could and slipped behind it. She drew the door completely shut and waited.

She had not long to wait. Steve's voice boomed through the silence.

"How about a stirrup cup for a dry traveler?" he asked jovially.

"Steve, it's late," Irma protested.

The light went on in the living room. A dim reflection came to Myra through the keyhole and under the door.

"It's only a quarter to twelve," Steve objected.

"I know but—I really think you should go. It doesn't look well—"

"Well, Madam Grundy!" He roared with laughter. It was evident that this drink would not be his first of the evening, by many. "The place is lousy with my chairs but I mayn't sit in 'em."

"That's very poor taste, Steve," she said coldly.

"Right. I withdraw the chairs. Merely a thirsty man's temper."

"You'll last till you get upstairs, I hope," she said tartly. Myra could hear the impatience and nervousness in her voice.

"You've got a heart of pure Italian marble, or is it just ice?"

"Steve, I told you at the Griers', I had a headache. Do run along. I want to take an aspirin and try to sleep."

"You're sure it's an aspirin you're chasing me for?"

"Please, Steve. I'm not in the mood for nonsense." Her patience was wearing paper-thin.

"You've changed a good bit since seven o'clock," he said slowly. "What were you then—defenseless, susceptible? By God, you're as susceptible now as Mont Blanc. What's happened to you?"

"Nothing at all. Didn't you ever have a headache?" Her voice began to vibrate with anger. "Get out, do you hear me!"

"All right, my lovely, I'll go—if you'll kiss me good night."

"Blackmailer! Very well. On the cheek." With main effort, she forced her tone back to lightness.

But even in her closet, Myra could tell it was not on the cheek. She could hear Irma's smothered protest, crushed by his lips on hers.

"There, beautiful. And if I find it's not an aspirin you're dated up with—"

"Silly!" She managed to laugh.

Myra heard the lobby door open and close. She heard Irma's furious "Damned drunken pig!" then the girl's hurried footsteps into the bedroom, the slam of a drawer, the click of the light switch, and the close of the street door. Irma was gone.

In the dark, Myra took the gun out of her bag and slipped off the safety catch. She wondered what the exact time was. If it was close to twelve, there was a ghastly chance that Irma and Lester might meet face to face in the street. In her mind she followed Irma along the short block, as if she could will her to pass the bar before Lester came out. It seemed a long time since Irma had left. Was it because Lester was being extraordinarily careful, or were they even now comparing notes and pulling down her house of cards?

Without warning, the light clicked on again. It came, brighter now, under the closet door and through the keyhole. Whoever had come in, had done so without a sound. Myra waited, scarcely breathing. She heard footsteps and then, from the living room, someone whistling "I Got Plenty o' Nuthin'."

It was a favorite song of Lester's, and she recognized his peculiar, high, rather musical whistle. They had not met. Irma was safely stashed in the garage. Lester was here, entirely unsuspicious. Her plan was succeeding. A few minutes more and she would have done what she set out to do, destroy these two deadly enemies. Her life would be safe, her dignity untarnished, and her debt paid in full.

Slowly, she opened the closet door. The hall was alight, and the living room. Soundlessly, she moved along the wall toward the living room door. She could hear Lester's whistle plainly now, as well as his footsteps as he paced restlessly up and down the room. Just before she reached the door, she paused and waited as he marched down the room toward it. He reached the door and she stepped out into the doorway. From a distance of four feet, she shot him through the heart. He was dead before he reached the ground.

She had a violent impulse to empty the gun into his prostrate body, like the woman in Maugham's *The Letter*, but she knew she would not. This was no time for emotional release. Myra Hudson, the craftsman, the constructor of well-built plots, fictional and nonfictional, was in charge. Myra Hudson's brain told her that even one shot was risky enough, with only a single wall separating the room from the lobby. But again, as several times before in the last three days, she felt that the stars in their courses were working with her; it was July third, and already, here and there, overeager celebrators were setting off firecrackers. Her shot would cause no question among so many others.

Lester lay, graceful in death as in life, relaxed and superlatively handsome, in a pose of peace. No fear, no horror creased his face. Even the small .22 bullet had done little external damage to his immaculate dinner coat. But Myra scarcely looked at him. She had work to do. First of all, she took from her bag the crumpled paper bearing, in Lester's own writing, the little "speech" she had asked him to write down that morning. She threw it into a corner, near the desk. Then she went swiftly into the bedroom and replaced the gun in the Sherry candy box where she had found it yesterday afternoon.

She came back into the living room and knelt beside Lester. With steady hands, she found his key case, detached his key to Irma's apartment, and dropped it into her bag with her own. She pulled out his cigarette case and snapped it open. The alleged note from Irma was not there. Methodically, not allowing herself to get flustered, she went through his pockets, one by one. She did not find it. She searched again, this time, forcing her hand under his body so that she could reach the back pockets of his trousers. In the right pocket she found his small, flat moiré wallet, which he wore with evening clothes. The note was lying folded inside his paper money. She put it in her bag with the other things, left the lights on, and slipped out of the apartment by the street door.

Unhurriedly, but with lowered head, the blond wig half

covering her face, she walked back to her house. At the corner, she stripped off her gloves and threw them through the grating of the sewer opening. After them, she sent the two keys and the scraps of the forged note. She let herself softly into her house and sped noiselessly up to her room.

It was over. Her plan had succeeded brilliantly. There were one or two more things to do—important things—but she had plenty of time. It was 12:25. Irma would stick to her post in the garage until one. Thirty-five minutes. Then she would go home. Whatever she did after she discovered Lester's body, Myra could count on a further delay, say an hour in all. Plenty of time.

She discovered that she was trembling violently and covered with cold perspiration. She went to the small built-in bar in the corner of her room and poured herself a generous drink. With the glass halfway to her lips she stopped. Perhaps the liquor had been tampered with, awaiting just some such moment as this, when she would take a drink alone and unsuspectingly. She would take no chances, now, when everything was working so perfectly. She went into Lester's room and without turning on a light—his room faced the back and consequently, the garage—groped for the flask which always stood on his bed table. She took a long drink from the flask and then, in the darkness, edged to the window and peered down at the garage. The doors were pulled to, and she could see nothing of Irma.

She went back to her room, undressed, and put on the same nightgown she had worn earlier. She pulled off the yellow wig and carried it and the box of grease paints up to the attic. Feeling her way in the dark, she stuffed them back into the trunk.

Back again in her room, she went over the list she had memorized and then burned that morning. The cylinders were the first item she considered. She wanted desperately to go down to her study and smash them but caution held her back. If she had left one tiny incriminating clue to her presence in Irma's apartment, she would need the cylinders badly. Again, suppose Irma had met someone—even a stranger who would remember that unforgettable face—on her way to the garage. Any doubt on the part of the police of Irma's guilt would lead to an intensive investigation of other solutions to the crime. She was well-advised to wait a day or two before destroying the cylinders. After all, nobody but Eve ever touched them and Eve had strict orders not to disturb them. Besides, Eve was away.

The second item was also debatable. Should she or should she not destroy all samples of Lester's writing that she could find? If Irma had destroyed the alleged note from Lester, there was no need to do so. But if she had kept it, as a sort of hold over him, it would be compared to examples of Lester's writing, found in his room. The note would be proved a forgery. Irma would escape punishment. But Myra believed that Irma's first act would be to destroy the note, because of the insidious line in it—*A thousand times better than your poison*— the line Myra had included deliberately for just this purpose. Then, too, and vastly important, it was necessary for the police to find samples of Lester's writing, in order to compare them to the crumpled note, actually in his own script. With the note repudiating Irma and declaring he was in love with his own wife pronounced genuine, the case against Irma was black and Myra's status as a beloved wife, preserved. She decided against destroying Lester's papers.

She drew a long breath. She had one more task to perform, the last link, and the chain would be complete. This was the hardest—or at least, the trickiest—of all the tricky things she had had to do tonight. She shrank from it with a shudder. Her firm, muscular little body had always been a good servant. She had rarely been ill and she hated physical pain. But it had to be done. Firmly, she went into the guest room and crossed to the window. The shade was up and a panorama of the East River and Long Island spread before her, softly illuminated by the lights from the Queensborough Bridge. With the window pole, she pushed the heavy window all the way up, and set down the pole close at hand. She pulled open the vanity drawer and took out the big shears. The window sill was no more than two feet from the floor. She raised her left leg until her ankle lay flat on the sill. With the shears in her hand, she reached over and cut at the heavy rope which held the window up. The shears were sharp but the tightly woven rope was tough. She had, practically, to gnaw her way through it with the blades. Laboriously she got through the first rope. The window held. She went to work on the second rope. Suddenly the frayed fibers parted. The window shot down like lightning on her bare ankle.

She thought she was going to die. Never in her life had she felt anything like the excruciating pain that began like a living flame in her ankle and spread in waves all through her body. She sagged against the glass, her stomach churning with nausea. For long minutes, she stood, like some grotesque stork on one leg, the other pinned under the intolerable weight of the window. Blindly, she groped for the window pole, crowding back screams of agony. She got it at last, and after a dozen fumbling attempts, propped it up under the top frame and pushed upward. She could not budge it. She clung to the pole and began to cry. Her tears gave way to a passionate fury and she pounded the window with one fist like an enraged child. The heavy plate glass did not even rattle. All thought of caution, of discovery, vanished. Nothing mattered but to be free of this monster that was crushing her.

She hung limply against the glass for a while, sweat streaming from every pore, her breath coming in rasps from her raw throat. At last, she gathered strength enough to steady the pole again and heaved upward until the veins of her neck stood out like ropes. This time, the window gave a couple of inches, and she dragged her ankle through the opening. She pitched forward in a dead faint, the window pole clattering to the floor beside her.

She regained consciousness, moaning with pain. But her mind was clear now, and she realized that at all costs, she must get back to her room. She shook her head, like a dog coming out of the water. There was something—the shears —the pole—

Somehow, she managed to prop the pole against the window. Then she felt around for the shears. She located them and crawled to the vanity table and dropped them into the open drawer. It took her five minutes to push the drawer shut.

Desperately, she began the terrible trip back to her room. Her left leg was worse than useless. As she pushed herself forward by her other knee and her hands, the wounded ankle scraped along the floor, convulsing her with torture. Three times she fainted for a brief, merciful period, but always the racking pain broke through and brought her back to agonized consciousness.

At long last, she found herself on the floor beside her bed, struggling like a mountain climber to raise herself. With one last, dreadful effort, she hurled her body up and into the bed, a quivering heap, half-mad with pain. The trip had taken her the best part of an hour.

She never knew how long she lay there, but finally the urgency of the moment forced her to further action. With slow careful movements, she disposed her body into an ordinary position in the bed. Her right foot—luckily, the sound one—struck against something cold. It was the towel-wrapped ice bag Austin had brought her, centuries ago, before this agony had begun to devour her.

She reached up and snapped on the small bed light attached to the headboard. She looked at the clock. It was sixteen minutes past one. Irma would be gone now. It was safe to have a light and she must examine the damage to her ankle and repair the disorder of her whole person as far as she could. Her evening bag lay on the bed table where she had dropped it an hour ago. She took out the mirror and looked at herself. She hardly recognized the dirt-and-tear-streaked face that looked back at her. The bloodshot eyes were glaring with suffering, and the thin upper lip was drawn back in an animal grin like a snarl. With her right foot, she worked up the ice bag in the bed until she got hold of it. She unscrewed the cap with unsteady fingers and dipped a corner of the towel into the melted ice. She wiped off her face, hands, and forearms and ran the comb through her hair. She brushed the dust off the front of her nightgown without much success but her blue chiffon bed jacket lay within reach and she slipped it on, hiding the soiled nightgown beneath it.

There remained her ankle to inspect. She sat up and began dragging the dead weight of her left leg toward her. She had laid the inner side of her ankle against the window sill, so that it was the outside which bore the brunt of the smashing blow. She leaned over and pulled back the sheet. A cry of pure horror escaped her. The ankle was swollen twice its natural size but what appalled her was the deep gaping two-inch-long cut that ran across it. It had evidently bled copiously because rivulets of black dried blood were glued to her ankle, instep, and heel. Somewhere along the Calvary from the guest room to her own, it had evidently stopped bleeding, because there were only one or two dim brown smears on the lower sheet. The upper one was mercifully unstained.

Again she dipped a corner of the towel into the ice bag and began to wipe the dirt and blood away from the wound. The lightest touch was agony. She gritted her teeth and went doggedly ahead. Her tortured breath whistled through her dilated nostrils, her fingers shook from the excruciating pain. But she did finally clean away the blood and dirt and wiped off her grimy knees. The cut gaped up at her like an ugly laughing mouth.

She could not turn the foot at all, it had no power of its own, beyond that of sending the racking pain to her nerves. With her two hands, she grasped her whole foot and with a desperate effort, turned it so that the cut lay against the mattress and only the swollen inner side of the ankle was visible. The struggle exhausted her and she had to lie back for a few minutes, fighting off her nausea and weakness.

She managed to stuff the damp filthy bloody towel between the mattress and the box spring. She could do no more. Trembling uncontrollably, she fumbled on the bed table for the sleeping tablets. With relief, she found them as well as the half-glass of stale water which still stood there from earlier in the evening. She swallowed two tablets and drained the warmish water greedily. She fell back on her pillows, utterly spent, her body aflame with pain.

CHAPTER XXIV

For nearly half an hour, Irma stood behind the garage door, her eye fixed to the narrow opening between the two loosely-closed leaves of the door. Her shining satin dress and silver wrap were folded over her shoulders, shawl-fashion. She was irritated that Steve's importunities had delayed her so long that she had been unable to change into something dark before dashing out of her apartment. But her real anger was directed against Lester. Never a patient person, she was chafing at the delay. Where was he? Why couldn't he be on time? What was this foolproof scheme he had on tap, anyway? His note sounded like something out of Roy Rogers or Superman. If she hadn't been so desperate, when her plans for getting Myra at the Grier dinner had been balked, she wouldn't have dreamed of coming. As if a lamebrain like Lester could devise anything really effective. But time was getting alarmingly short. Tomorrow would be Friday, and Monday that damnable will would be executed. She was in a mood to try anything. But what could he have in mind? Probably some idiotic plot to frame Myra's death to look like murder and robbery. No doubt he wanted Irma there to tie him up, like in that Long Island case—Judd Gray and Ruth Snyder. It hadn't taken the police long to get to the bottom of *that* fake. Well, she wanted no part of any such setup. Too many things could go wrong, and she had no intention of paying any penalty when she got rid of Myra.

If only Lester showed up now, something might still be done tonight. If she could persuade Lester to take enough of the poison to make him really ill but not kill him they would find ways to force a fatal dose on Myra, especially tonight with her bad ankle. Then he'd be in the clear, it would look like something the two of them had eaten or drunk at home—a case of accidental poison—

The thought reminded her again of Lester's stupidity. Only a dimwit would have put the word "poison" on paper. Well, she sure got rid of that in a hurry, down Alice's toilet. But every line of it stood out in her memory. *Tonight or never*. That must mean while Myra was tied to her bed on account of her ankle. But wait a minute—the only time Lester could have slipped the note into her compact was when he stood behind her at the console table. And that was *before* Myra had sprained her ankle. What *was* his idea, anyway?

She began to get tired. She moved back from the door and sat down in Lester's Cadillac. In the dim light coming through the garage window from the street, she noticed that only the Cadillac and Myra's Chrysler were in the garage. There was an empty space where the secretary's car usually stood. Probably out for a ride to get away from the heat. Maybe Lester knew Eve was out for the evening and figured it was a good time for action on that account.

She opened her bag and brought out a man's wristwatch with a luminous dial. Twelve-thirty-five. The idiot! That was another thing. Telling her so jauntily in his note to go home at one o'clock. How the hell did he think she was going to *know* when it was one o'clock in a dark garage? Just because she had foresight enough to bring along her father's old watch was no excuse for him. Well, the dumber he was, the easier he'd be to handle later.

She'd handle him, all right. When the time came, he'd figure in a sure-enough accident. It would be a cinch. The fool couldn't swim. And what a widow she'd make—black against her creamy skin. But first, there was Myra to take care of, then Lester had to cash in, then her marriage to him—the quicker the better, as far as she was concerned. What she wanted was to get her hands on real money. It would be fun to own a stable, to see your colors parade to the post, to know when your horse was out for air and when you could really put the checks down. She didn't know how you went about acquiring a stable, but Steve could help her there. Even after she married Lester, she must keep Steve hanging around. He was useful in a lot of ways. She had to watch her step in future. She nearly slipped tonight, losing her temper with him. That was one thing she'd have to learn—to control that red-rage temper of hers when she was crossed. But she just couldn't help it. She loathed drunks and above all, she loathed being mauled. She couldn't bear to be touched. Of course, this greedy masculine yen that they all had for her gave her a good handle. Men made her sick altogether, but she'd have to grin and bear it until she was sitting pretty.

Ten minutes to one and still no Lester. Was it some kind of a plant? Could he be crossing her up? With his birdbrain, could he have doped out some scheme with her as the goat? No, he was too crazy in love with her for anything like that. Maybe he had carried Myra down here, stuck her in the Chrysler and settled her hash with monoxide gas. He'd had the whole evening to do it in. Then, just *because* he was so nuts about her, he'd want her to be in on it as deep as he was. He'd figure that in a whole hour, her fingerprints would be smeared all over the garage. If that was his idea, she had fooled him, but good. From the minute she'd opened the garage doors, she'd been extra careful to use a handkerchief on whatever she touched. If Myra was dead in the Chrysler, there wasn't a thing to connect *her* with it. But it was all out of line. He didn't have the brains or the guts to carry out such a plan. The answer was some cockeyed idea like the murder-robbery business and either he got cold feet or wasn't able to come downstairs to her.

Could be that he really couldn't get away. If Myra's sore ankle kept her awake, you could be damn sure she was keeping him on the jump, cracking her whip, ordering him around, making him earn every dime she handed out. How she hated her, with her I'm-God-and-you're-a-worm air. It'd be a pleasure to kill her, to show her who really *was* God. If only she could feed her the poison and then, when she was helpless but still conscious, let her know how pretty boy Lester felt about her! That would be really something, to watch her damned pride shrivel—

Suddenly, Irma ducked down on the seat of the Cadillac. Two brilliant pencils of light struck the back wall of the garage, and a car came rolling in. She lay suffocating with fright, her heartbeats almost drowning out the motor in her ears. Then the motor was turned off, leaving a silence that made her afraid to breathe. She heard the car door close softly, then the sound of light retreating footsteps, but no words. Then, to her horror, the unmistakable click as someone pressed the hasp of the padlock into place.

She crept out of the Cadillac and went to the garage doors. Now, more than ever careful to veil her fingers in her handkerchief, she pushed against the doors. They were firmly in place and did not give an inch.

A flood of rage swept over her. She raised her arms in an insensate urge to pound madly on the solid wood and to scream at the top of her lungs. Only just in time, she stopped herself. A cold calculating film of ice cooled her blood. She stood weighing the situation, her beautiful lips closed in a calm, deadly anger, much more dreadful than any show of temper.

She relaxed and almost smiled. The window, of course. It was close to the ground, she could practically step out of it. Carefully, she got it open, still watchful to leave no prints. When she was outside, she closed it again noiselessly.

CHAPTER XXV

As Irma unlocked her street door, she noticed, with faint surprise, the light seeping through the crevices of the Venetian blinds. She thought she had turned them off when she left.

She closed the door and went into the lighted living room. Lester lay on his back, his open eyes staring at the ceiling. Enough blood had spread to form a stiff dark-brown spot on his white shirt. Irma gave a loud panic-stricken scream and tore through the other door into the lobby of the building.

"Help! Help! Come quick!"

The doorman came running from the front and the elevator boy from the rear. She waved them to follow her and they all crowded into her living room.

"Jesus God!" said the doorman and crossed himself. Jimmy was of different mettle.

"Holy cow! A sure-enough stiff! What gives?"

"I don't know. I just came in and found him," Irma gibbered. "Do something! Get somebody!"

Jimmy, a hardboiled whodunit fan, knew exactly what to do. He went back to the lobby, noted the time, called Spring 7-3100, and asked for Homicide.

"Send up the works, pronto. A guy's been rubbed out with a heater up here in a doll's joint. No weapon. Looks like a frying job." He gave the address and identified himself.

In five minutes, a radio car whined to a stop before the door, and its two occupants stabilized the situation until H.Q. people arrived. Twenty minutes later, three cars parked behind the radio car, and seven men poured into Irma's little apartment.

The men from the radio car gave Captain Croy of Homicide the bare facts, gathered from Jimmy and Irma; the name of the dead man, the girl's name, and the time of discovery—1:12 a.m. The girl had passed out—or faked it, they weren't sure which—so they couldn't get more. She was just coming to, now.

Croy was a good-looking, severe thirty-seven, a man who loved his work and was good at it. He turned to Irma who was lying back on the couch, pale and incredibly beautiful.

"You are—"

"Irma Neves." She was under control now but fighting her fright.

"Miss or Mrs.?"

"Miss."

"This is your apartment?"

"Yes."

"And the—" He nodded toward Lester.

"Lester Blaine."

"A friend of yours?"

"Yes—actually my friend's husband."

"That is, you and *Mrs.* Blaine?"

"That's right."

"What was he doing here?"

"I have no idea."

"How is that?"

"I just came in and—found him."

"Where had you been?"

"Out."

"Out where?"

"Just walking."

Croy's cool eyes took in her full-length white satin dress, the silver wrap on the arm of the couch, her high-heeled silver slippers. He said nothing, but Irma was immediately on the defensive. She swung her feet down from the couch and sat up.

"I had been out to a party earlier. After I got home, I had this headache and I thought a breath of air would do me good."

Bendix, the medical officer, was kneeling beside Lester. Two men were puffing white powder on dark surfaces and dark powder on light surfaces. The cameraman and his assistant were unfolding a tripod and getting out flashbulbs. Sergeant Klein, Croy's assistant, was ranging through the rooms, touching nothing, merely using his eyes. In a straight chair, Daly, a young blond cop, was taking shorthand notes. The two radio-car men prepared to leave. Jimmy, the elevator boy, and Ryan, the doorman, took it all in, bug-eyed.

"What time was this?" asked Croy.

"I got home from the party before twelve."

"Can you be a little more specific?"

"Well, I would say, twenty minutes to twelve."

"And you went out again at—"

"Five minutes to twelve."

"You seem sure of that."

"Yes. I looked at the time as I went out."

Croy's eyes went around the room. There was no clock. "Where did you see the time?"

Irma opened her bag and brought out the wristwatch. "By this."

Croy took it to compare it to his own. At the same time, with an absent air, he reached for her evening bag. For a moment, Irma made nothing of this, then suddenly, every trace of color left her face. She made a quick motion to recover the bag. Croy, surprised, but equal to the occasion, stepped back just far enough to be out of her reach. Then, casually, as if nothing significant had struck him, he went on.

"Do you always carry a man's watch to a party, Miss Neves?"

With a striking effort, she recovered herself.

"No—I—it was on my bureau— When I went for my walk, I took it along."

"I see. At five minutes to twelve, you picked up the watch and went for a walk."

"Yes."

"The deceased—Mr. Blaine—was not here then?"

"No."

"Where did you go?"

"I—just walked. It was so warm—I knew I couldn't sleep—"

"You didn't drop in anywhere—say a bar—or see anyone you knew?"

"No."

"And you returned home at—"

"A few minutes after one, I think."

"One-twelve," Jimmy put in. "I looked when I called Homicide."

"That was quite a breath of air," said Croy equably. "One hour and seventeen minutes."

"I told you I had a headache. I still have. If you'll please let me have my bag, I'd like to take an aspirin."

Bendix, the M.O., raised his head.

"Death occurred between one and a half and two hours ago, I judge," he said.

Croy glanced at Irma's watch, which he still held. He said, "It's one forty-five now. That would make it somewhere between a quarter to twelve and a quarter past. Right?"

Negligently, he handed the watch and the bag to Klein, as the sergeant wandered by him. Croy covertly watched Irma's eyes. There was panic in them, and he could not understand why. The bag was too small and too light to hold a gun. Well, Klein would know what to do.

Bendix replied, "Don't hold me to the minute. I'll know better after I do the post. Even so, there's always a margin."

"But he *could* have been shot at eleven forty-five?"

"Easily."

"That's ridiculous!" said Irma loudly. "Why, I was here with Mr. Thatcher then."

"Oh?" said Croy.

"Certainly. Mr. Stephen Thatcher. The owner of this building. He'll tell you."

"Right," Jimmy volunteered. "He came outa here to the lobby and I took him up."

"Up?"

"He lives on the roof. Penthouse."

"What time was that?"

"Around when the lady says." A note of deep regret crept into Jimmy's voice. "I didn't look at the time, but I figure five or ten to twelve."

"Do you agree, Miss Neves?"

"Yes, that's about right."

"And between ten to twelve and five to twelve, you are sure Mr. Blaine did not appear?"

"Of course not. It wasn't more than a minute or two before I left, myself."

Croy dropped a whispered word to Sergeant Klein.

Klein nodded and went out the lobby door, while Croy turned to Jimmy.

"You and Ryan had better get back to your posts. I'll talk to you later if I need you."

Reluctantly, Jimmy led the way back to duty.

Irma immediately went on. "Mr. Thatcher can tell you I had a headache. And that he—Mr. Blaine wasn't here then."

"How do you account for the fact that he was here when you returned?"

"I can't."

"You didn't leave your door open?"

"Oh, no."

"Perhaps he had a key?"

"Not to my knowledge. Why should he?"

"There was no one else here to let him in?"

"No. I live alone."

"How about the windows?"

"They're always locked. The apartment is air-cooled."

"Well—Miss Neves, where was this party you attended?"

"At Mr. and Mrs. Tony Griers'. They live at Eleventh Street and Fifth Avenue." Croy raised mental eyebrows. First, the name of Steve Thatcher had lifted the case out of the ordinary love nest shooting class. And now Mr. and Mrs. Tony Grier, real top-drawer New Yorkers. If this gorgeous creature wasn't spinning fairy tales, Croy was facing something formidable. Irma continued. "It wasn't a big party. Just six of us—that is—"

"Yes?"

"Originally it was dinner and bridge for eight, but Mr. and

Mrs. Blaine had to call it off at the last minute."

"Why was that?"

"Mr. Thatcher and I called for them at seven. We were just going to have a cocktail when Mrs. Blaine sprained her ankle. She couldn't stand on it, and Mr. Blaine wouldn't go without her."

"They sound a very devoted couple."

"Oh, very." Croy listened for overtones in the short answer. He found none.

"Where do they live?"

"Sutton Place. Just a block from here."

"When you took your—walk, did you pass their house?"

"No, I walked south."

"How far?"

"I didn't notice."

"You're quite sure that somewhere on your way, you didn't—ah—chance to meet Mr. Blaine and bring him back with you?"

"I'm *quite* sure," she said curtly.

A clang outside announced the arrival of the morgue wagon. Croy turned to the men who had been busy at their various jobs.

"Got all the pictures you need, London?"

"Yes, Cap."

"Harris, how about his prints?"

"Took 'em first thing."

"You finished with him, Doc?"

"Yes. I can't do any more here. Bullet's still in him. I'll get that downtown for Ballistics."

As the two husky young men came in with a stretcher, Croy nodded to them. "Take it away, boys."

Croy noticed that Irma watched the whole procedure of getting the dead man onto the stretcher and out of the house. Not a muscle of her exquisite face changed.

The room was normal again when Sergeant Klein returned through the lobby door followed by Steve Thatcher.

Steve had evidently not been to bed as he was still in his dinner clothes. Evidently, too, the effect of his evening's drinks had worn off completely. He was cold sober.

Steve was well known at police headquarters, if not too popular. He had defended and won acquittals for many men whom the police had worked hard to track down.

Croy had met him personally and did not minimize the lawyer's ability or importance.

"Hello, Captain," said Steve.

"How are you, Mr. Thatcher?"

"What goes on?"

"A little trouble here in Miss Neves's apartment. We just want you to check on certain times for us."

Steve grinned.

"First time I've been asked to testify *for* your department."

"I guess that's right, too. Now, if you'll just tell me when you brought Miss Neves home?"

Steve sobered.

"Captain, the fact that you're here at all, spells homicide. What the devil's happened?"

"Just answer my question, please. You'll find out in good time."

"Let's see— We left the Griers' at eleven-thirty. I should judge about a quarter to twelve. That help you any?"

"Near enough. Did you come in?"

"Yes. For a minute or two."

"Anybody else here at the time?"

"Nobody."

"You're sure you stayed only a minute or two?"

"Well, five at the outside. Miss Neves had a splitting headache and she couldn't get rid of me fast enough. She wanted to take an aspirin and go to bed."

"I see."

"That's true," Irma broke in. "But I changed my mind—"

"All in good time, Miss Neves. I'll come back to you."

Steve gave Irma a long, considering look.

"Mr. Thatcher, do you know a Lester Blaine?"

"Lester? Of course. He's Myra Hudson's husband."

"Steve, tell him—" Irma cut in hotly.

"Klein! Take Miss Neves into the bedroom."

Irma curbed her rising anger. "I'm sorry, Captain. I won't

interrupt anymore," she begged.

"All right, Miss Neves. But if it happens again—"

Klein, who had stopped his prowling at Croy's order, went back to his seemingly casual search.

"You mean *the* Myra Hudson?" Croy asked Steve, as if there had been no break in the questioning.

"Yes."

"Blaine was shot to death in this room between eleven forty-five and twelve-fifteen tonight."

"Good God!"

Again his eyes sought Irma's. She was leaning toward him, her whole soul in her gaze. There was innocence in her wide eyes, and desperate appeal. And with these two, she somehow managed to blend promise, personal and intoxicating. He had never seen her look more beautiful.

Croy's voice broke in on him.

"You say Miss Neves couldn't get rid of you fast enough?"

"Oh, that was just a manner of speaking. She asked me to go because she had a headache."

"Could it be that she wanted you to leave because she was expecting another visitor?"

"There was absolutely no indication of any such idea."

"But from her attitude, that *might* have been the case?"

"Knowing Miss Neves—*and* Blaine—I am positive it was *not* the case."

"How well did you know Blaine?"

"Only casually, since his marriage. But enough to know that he had eyes only for his wife."

"How long have they been married?"

"Something more than a year, I believe."

"And, you say, happily married?"

"Unquestionably. Strikingly. All the more so because Blaine is—was—somewhat younger than his wife."

"Then you would consider it unlikely that Blaine had a rendezvous here with Miss Neves tonight?"

"I would consider it ridiculous."

"Have you ever observed Miss Neves and Blaine together?"

"Often. I never saw anything more than the most casual

politeness between them. As I said, if Blaine wasn't utterly devoted to his wife, he was the world's best actor."

Sergeant Klein came to Croy and whispered to him.

The two men stepped into the little hall out of sight of the living room. Irma made an impulsive gesture.

"Steve! Please!"

He raised a hand, shook his head, and indicated Daly, the police stenographer.

Croy returned, gingerly holding a crumpled paper by one corner.

"Mr. Thatcher, I am going to read you a note. I want to know if you think it possible that Blaine wrote it."

"Let's have it."

"'My dear girl, if you can be uninhibited, so can I. You say you love me and make no bones about it. Can you take it as well as dish it? Well, I *don't* love you. If you think me a heel, get this—it happens I'm in love with my wife.'"

Irma stamped her foot. "This is some plot—" she began furiously.

"Irma! Shut up!" Steve snapped.

"I won't! These are a lot of lies—"

"Klein!"

Klein took her arm and propelled her, protesting, into the bedroom.

Croy said, "Well, Mr. Thatcher?"

A muscle ticked in Steve's jaw, but he said lightly, "The note is hardly congruous with a guilty rendezvous, Captain, would you say?"

"No, but it contains material for an excellent motive for murder."

"The Hell-hath-no-fury theme? But you'd have to jump a barrier. Granting Blaine is this self-righteous Joseph, how do you place him in the apartment of Potiphar's wife at midnight?"

"That's easy—one last meeting to say good-by—any of a dozen dodges a clever woman could think up."

"Captain, aren't you going at this thing wrong? Before jumping to conclusions, hadn't you better locate the weapon, for instance?"

"Our technique is fairly comprehensive," he said dryly.

"And find out where Miss Neves was at the time of the crime?"

"Miss Neves claims she was out for a walk."

"Why should you doubt it?"

"Does it seem reasonable that a lady in evening clothes paraded the streets from eleven fifty-five to one-twelve alone and for the sole purpose of getting rid of a headache?"

"You will have a tough time disproving it, Captain."

"I gather that you expect to represent Miss Neves?"

"If she requests it, I am at her disposal. Captain," he added gravely, "don't ruin that girl's future by a hasty arrest."

"I haven't arrested her yet."

"You're treating her like a criminal."

"No, only like a suspect."

"Look, I know all these people well. It's utterly ridiculous that she should have killed Myra Hudson's husband!"

"I would be grateful for any enlightenment you can give me."

"In the first place, Miss Neves owes not only her present social position but actually her life to Myra Hudson."

"How is that?"

"Myra rescued her from drowning. Later, she developed a liking for her, took her under her wing, and introduced her to society. Only a monster would repay such kindness by stealing her benefactor's husband. Miss Neves is no monster."

"No, she is a remarkably beautiful woman, I noticed," returned Croy cynically.

Steve shrugged.

"I see your mind is made up, Captain. But as Miss Neves's voluntary representative, I warn you I can shoot your case so full of holes, you'll never get an indictment. Meanwhile you smear an innocent girl for life. I want to avoid that."

"Have you any alternate theory to offer?"

"There should be any number."

"Such as?"

"I'm not a detective, Captain."

"Would you consider the dead man's wife a likelihood?"

"I would not."

"How is that?"

"Even given the improbability of an affair between Blaine and Miss Neves, Myra Hudson wouldn't stoop to murder as a solution. It is totally out of character, even if she could have done so, physically, which she could not."

"Anyone can fire a gun."

"She would have to be on the spot first. It happens that I was present early this evening when Mrs. Blaine tripped on a flight of stairs and sprained her ankle badly. She couldn't stand on it, much less walk over here."

"A sprained ankle could be faked."

"Not this one. I saw it."

"And?"

"It was angry and inflamed within two minutes."

Croy mulled over this for a few moments but made no comment. Then he observed, "That hardly helps Miss Neves's case, would you say?"

"No, but this does—she is an extraordinarily intelligent girl. If she had killed Blaine, do you think she'd be fool enough to leave that preposterous note around, to be picked up by the police? It's obviously the crudest sort of plant."

"We'll find that out when we check the handwriting and fingerprints. If Blaine did write it, I can picture a situation where Miss Neves's intelligence would be so clouded by jealousy and anger that she could have crumpled it up and tossed it furiously in a corner, and later, under stress of emotion, forgotten all about it."

"Which do you go for, Captain?" Steve asked suavely. "Poirot or Perry Mason?" Croy reddened under the sarcasm. "Meanwhile, until you find the weapon, or other evidence than the figments of an active imagination, I protest against your treating Miss Neves like a convicted criminal."

Croy did not reply. Instead, he called, "Klein! Bring Miss Neves in."

Irma came in. It was plain that she was seething inwardly but controlling it with every scrap of will power she could summon. She was beginning to realize that, for once, she was pitted against a man who had eyes, not for beauty but for facts.

"Miss Neves," asked Croy. "Do you own a gun?"

"No, of course not—"

Steve raised his head sharply and looked at her. Her hand went to her throat, and she caught her breath.

"Oh—that is—"

"Yes, Miss Neves?"

"There—is one here—Mr. Thatcher left it the other day—"

"How was that?"

"He—thought I'd feel safer—the ground floor—" Suddenly naked rage showed in her eyes as she turned toward Steve. "I *told* you to take it away—*I* didn't want the thing—"

"Where is this gun, Miss Neves?"

"In the bedroom closet." Her tone was sullen.

Croy's eyes met Klein's. The sergeant left the room. In a moment, small tumbling noises could be heard from the bedroom.

"Miss Neves, would you recognize Blaine's writing if you saw it?"

"No. I never saw it. Can't I make you understand? There was nothing—absolutely nothing—between us. I don't think he even liked me. I tell you, no woman in the world existed for him except his wife." The words came in a rush.

"His note makes that quite clear."

"Note! You can't believe he actually *wrote* that—I never saw that note before—somebody deliberately—Captain, you've *got* to believe me—"

"Now, if you'll clarify *your* feeling for him—" said Croy imperturbably. Irma gasped with the realization that she could make no emotional headway with him.

"My feeling! I didn't care if he lived or died—" She caught herself up at the unfortunate locution. "I mean—I didn't care a—a straw for him—he meant *nothing* to me. This whole thing is a plot—somebody's trying to get me—"

"You are implying that someone hates you enough to pick off Blaine like a clay pigeon merely to pin the crime on you?"

"That's just what I mean. *I* didn't do it."

"Can you suggest any such enemy?"

"I can't. But it's plain, isn't it?"

Klein came in. He had a pencil in his hand. On the pencil swung a small blue automatic.

"Got it, Cap," he said. Croy went close and sniffed. "Yep. Been fired tonight or I'm a toe dancer. Whole closet stinks of it."

"This the gun Mr. Thatcher presented you with, Miss Neves?"

"I—suppose so—but if it's been fired—"

"Harris!" called Croy. The fingerprint man appeared from the kitchen.

"Yes, Captain?"

"Drop what you're doing. Get the prints on that gun."

"Right! Smells like the baby that did the trick."

He took hold of the pencil on which the gun hung and went back to the kitchen.

"Of course my fingerprints will be on it—" Irma began.

Klein cut in deliberately. "Another thing, Cap. There's enough poison in that bedroom closet to kill the Russian army."

"Captain—" said Irma desperately.

"Yes, Miss Neves?"

"Irma! Keep your mouth shut!" Steve ordered loudly.

"I won't!"

"Don't say another word!"

"I *want* to—"

"Do you hear me?"

"I've got to—"

"As your lawyer, I tell you to say nothing!"

"When you hear, you'll understand—I can explain the whole thing—"

"I advise you—"

"Leave me alone—I'm not standing for all this hocus-pocus—"

"You wish to amend your story, Miss Neves?" Croy put in gently.

"Yes, I do."

Steve dropped his hands in a gesture of despair.

"Captain, I admit—I haven't been entirely frank with you. I want to tell you the whole truth."

"You are wise, Miss Neves."

"I didn't at first. I was afraid it would sound too fantastic to be believed. But now—"

"We hear a good many fantastic things that are true."

"Well—first of all, that stuff in the closet—there is poison—among other things. It's all just certain supplies that were in my father's dental cabinet. I—I wasn't too affluent after his death—I thought I could sell them to some other dentist—and then I forgot all about them."

"I see."

"Now, about tonight. I really did go out right after Mr. Thatcher left. But not just for a walk—or because I had a headache—"

"Go on."

"Here's what happened. When I got to the Griers' tonight, I opened my compact to freshen my make-up. There was a note in it. It told me to go to the Blaines' garage at exactly twelve o'clock."

"For what purpose?"

Irma swallowed. The delay was lost on neither Croy nor Steve.

"The note didn't say. But the tone was very urgent."

"You have this note?"

"N-No. It said to destroy it. But I know exactly what was in it. I was to wait until one o'clock, and if no one came, then I was to go home."

"And who wrote the note?"

"It wasn't signed but—"

"Yes?"

"I *have* seen Lester Blaine's handwriting. I thought it was from him. *Now* I'm not so sure."

Steve groaned.

Croy said mildly, "And believing it to be Blaine's writing, at his *urgent* behest, you followed his instructions and waited in a dark garage from midnight until one a.m.? Is that right?"

"I—I suppose it looks bad, but it isn't, really. Naturally, Lester and I were friendly. I was their house guest for weeks. There was never anything the least bit—wrong—but I—well, I've got a tremendous bump of curiosity—or daring, if you want to call it that. Captain, please believe me! I swear I did get this note and went to the garage and waited a full hour there. Now you see why I took the wristwatch along."

"Was your—curiosity rewarded?"

"Nobody came—nothing. Oh! Wait! Wait! Of course! I can *prove* I was there. While I waited—I even know the exact time—at ten minutes to one—Eve Taylor, Mrs. Blaine's secretary, drove into the garage. You can—"

"Irma! For God's sake! This is hopeless!" Steve expostulated. Irma turned on him furiously.

"What's the matter with you?" she cried shrilly. "Why shouldn't I clear myself? Let him ask Eve—why do you keep shutting me up?"

"Irma, Captain Croy has only to ask one question to discover that Eve is spending the weekend with the Streets on Long Island."

"I tell you I saw her—I know her Ford—"

"Miss Neves," Croy put in. "You say you found the note in your compact. Who had access to it?"

With an effort, Irma composed herself.

"Well, the Griers and the Masons—no, none of them. I never had my bag out of my hand there until I used the compact. It would have to be somebody at the Blaines'."

"How is that?"

"I used the compact at home, and there was no note in it. Then St—Mr. Thatcher came, and we called for the Blaines."

"That means Mr. Thatcher or Mr. or Mrs. Blaine could have slipped the note in? Anyone else?"

"No one. Mr. Blaine had a good chance; he was standing beside me, and my bag was on a table—I was quite sure he had done it. After one o'clock, when nobody came to the garage, I figured it was some silly practical joke of his. Now, I see it was a trick of the murderer to get me out of the way, while he killed Lester here and involved me."

"Did Mrs. Blaine have any opportunity to slip the note in?"

"Easily while we were up in her room."

"Can you suggest any motive?"

Irma's face brightened.

"She could have—misunderstood Lester's friendliness to me—after all, an older woman with a young good-looking husband—yes, if she were jealous—she's very clever—she could have done it to get me out of the way while she came over here—"

"Aren't you forgetting the fact that she couldn't very well come over here on account of her sprained ankle?"

"I'd investigate that sprained ankle, if I were you," she said insolently. "Instead of badgering me to death about something I don't know a thing about." One by one, the strands binding her temper were fraying and loosening.

"A good suggestion," he returned imperturbably. "Now, in your opinion, did Mr. Thatcher have any opportunity of slipping the note into your compact?"

Every muscle in her body tensed like a panther's as she turned and bored into Steve with eyes that were blue-black with cold fury.

"Did he? He had *two* chances. Here, and at the Blaines'. I'm beginning to see why he's trying so hard to head me off. *I* mustn't talk, *I* mustn't protect myself. Oh, no! I should let myself be led like a lamb to the slaughter—to save *his* hide!"

"And *his* motive, Miss Neves?"

"Motive! He's in love with me. I can't be five minutes with him without his begging me to marry him. If he thought there was anything between Lester and me— It's getting plainer every minute. *He* brought me that gun. *He* put the note in my bag. *He* faked that thing you read out loud— Why, of course! He owns this building. Naturally, he had a key to my apartment. It explains everything!" She was shaking from head to toe.

Steve laughed, a pleasant, genuine laugh. He shook his head with an odd doglike gesture as if he were clearing it of cobwebs. He said with quiet amusement, "Captain, the force has lost a great detective in Miss Neves. It's absolutely true; I *was* in love with her. I *did* ask her to marry me. I *did* give her the gun. And I *do* have access to a master key to all the apartments in the building. Her reconstruction of the crime is as sound as a bell. Except for one thing. On her own showing, I left her at ten minutes to twelve. Jimmy took me up to my apartment where His Honor, Judge Folsom, was waiting for me, to discuss a pressing legal matter. From five minutes to twelve until your man brought me down here, I was not out of Judge Folsom's sight for one second." He rose. Irma's face was ashen. She made a half-movement toward him, but he ignored it. "I think my usefulness down here is practically nil, so with your permission, Captain, I'll go back to my unfinished business with the Judge. God knows what he's doing all this time with my Scotch! You can always find me, if you want me."

He moved toward the door.

Irma cried, "Steve! Please! I don't know what I'm saying—I'm distracted—"

Steve kept right on going.

As he went through to the breakfast nook, Harris passed him and came into the living room. He was holding the gun.

"Prints on the gun check with those all over the place, Captain. One shot fired."

"Take Miss Neves's prints now."

"You can't do that!" she screamed. "I can refuse."

"You are under arrest, Miss Neves, on suspicion of murder. And one more question. Did you expect to make a sale of your father's effects at the Griers' tonight? Is that why you were carrying a quantity of arsenic in your handbag?"

CHAPTER XXVI

It was a quarter to three when Croy, leaving Daly on guard at the apartment, left for the Blaine house. He sent Klein to headquarters with Irma to book her on the suspicion-of-murder charge. Harris, the fingerprint man, he took with him to Myra's.

"What goes, Chief? You don't want me taking the widow's prints right when you break it to her, do you?"

"I want you to go through the Blaine garage with a fine-tooth comb. Especially the doors, car fenders—any surface a person might touch during an hour's wait in the dark. You might feel the Ford's radiator, too—see if it's warm, although after two hours, I don't suppose it's much use."

"Cap, you don't *believe* that dame's fish tale?"

"No, I don't. I think she's as guilty as hell. She's like a cornered rat trying to shove the blame on everybody within miles. And concocting one lie after another as fast as she can talk. But my opinion isn't evidence for the Grand Jury. When I bring in the case, I want to make it stick. So I've got to be able to swear there isn't a sign of her fingerprints in that garage to bear out her story."

"I get it. And if there *are* some prints of the babe's?"

"Then I've got to take her story a little more seriously. It *could* be true, cockeyed as it sounds. If a smart operator did want to pin it on her, he might work out just some such movie plot. This is no professional crime. And when amateurs pull a murder, God help us poor cops."

"Horsefeathers, Cap. We both know the fancier the scenario the more chance for slip-ups."

"Well—I guess we don't need to worry much. Her whole horse opera sounds like pure moonshine. The first thing she could lay her tongue to. Looks to me like she expected to polish Blaine off at the Griers' with that poison she had in her bag. Then, when he stayed at home with his wife, she got him over to her place late, somehow or other, and used the gun instead."

"Two to one I'll just be wasting powder in the garage."

"Yes, but I've got to cover all the angles. I'm here to break the news to the widow, but I'm checking on that ankle of hers, too."

"Jeez, Cap, how you gonna make it? Walk in cold and say, 'Lady, your husband's full of lead. Will you do me a favor and stroll around the room?'"

"I won't have to be quite that crude. But if I must, I will. You see, Thatcher said something that makes this ankle sequence sound kind of fishy."

"What was that, Chief?"

"He said it was angry and inflamed within two minutes. Well, it takes time for the congealed blood to push up to the surface. Unless it was a hell of a crack or she knocked it as well as turned it, no ankle would show a thing in two minutes."

"Nice going, Chief."

"If what Thatcher saw was true, by midnight the ankle would have been twice its size and unusable. That lets Mrs. Blaine out and narrows the field. Here we are. I'll rout out the house. You go right to the garage. If it's locked, come in and ask for the key."

It was a barbarous hour to rouse a household, but Croy rang the bell without a scruple. He had to ring it four times before a disheveled Austin, a terry cloth robe over his pajamas, opened the door.

Croy identified himself, and Austin let him in. "There's been an accident to Mr. Blaine. Before I see his wife, I want to ask a few questions."

"Yes, Inspector." Austin, the former Tenth Avenue kid had a holy horror of the police. He was painfully obsequious.

"Captain."

"Captain. Anything I can do—"

"I understand Miss Irma Neves and Mr. Stephen Thatcher were here this evening around seven."

"That is so, Captain."

"How long were they here?"

"Not above twenty minutes, Captain. They were picking up Mr. and Mrs. Blaine and all going on to a dinner. Mr. Blaine mixed a cocktail but it was never drunk, owing to the mishap to Mrs. Blaine's ankle."

"Were you present during that time?"

"Yes, Captain. At the exact moment that she fell, I was pouring out the cocktails, not five feet away."

"If you were pouring out the cocktails, you didn't actually *see* her fall. Is that right?"

"Technically, yes. But it was only a matter of seconds before we all turned to her. And we all saw the damage."

"You mean to the ankle?"

"Yes, Captain."

"Just describe the damage."

"It looked bad, Captain."

"Swollen?"

"Well, no, sir. But rather discolored—not actually red—livid, I should say, describes it."

"How soon after she fell did you see it?"

"Two or three minutes, perhaps. She sat on the bottom step—then tried to stand on it—no—before she tried that, she turned up her skirt and we all saw it. Two or three minutes at the outside."

"Then what happened?"

"Mr. Blaine carried her up to bed. Then he telephoned to cancel the dinner appointment."

"It must have been really bad."

"Too bad for her to step on, yes, sir."

"And Blaine stayed at home, too?"

"Oh, yes, sir. He would never have left her alone."

"Devoted husband, eh?"

"Indeed, Captain. A pair of turtledoves, if I may offer an opinion."

"So I understand. Now, when did the doctor come?"

"Doctor? He didn't, Captain. Mrs. Blaine wouldn't have him in."

"But if the ankle was as bad as you say—"

"Mrs. Blaine, if I may be permitted to say so, is a lady of a good deal of pluck and self-control. She pooh-poohed the whole thing—begged Mr. Blaine to go without her—and absolutely refused to have in the doctor."

"What happened then?"

"I brought them up a sort of scratch meal and, about three quarters of an hour later, came and cleared it away."

"It is one of your duties to prepare dinner?"

"Oh, no, Captain. But owing to the fact that Mr. and Mrs. Blaine were dining out, the cook, Mrs. Link, and the second maid, Lily, had already left for the night."

"And after you cleared away?"

"It was then about nine-thirty. I listened to the wireless a short time and then retired."

"Where is your room?"

"Next to the kitchen, sir."

"Then Mr. Blaine might have left the house after nine-thirty without your hearing him?"

"Oh, easily, Captain. My quarters are at the back of the house."

"Now, Austin, Miss Neves was a house guest here, I understand. What sort of person did you make her to be?"

"Very beautiful, sir."

"Yes. I mean, what were her relations here in the house?"

"Very pleasant, sir."

"With both Mr. and Mrs. Blaine?"

"Yes, sir."

"Can you enlarge on that a trifle?"

"Well, sir, I am not wholly unobservant. If you want my private view—"

"That's just what I do want."

"I think Miss Neves a very cool customer, indeed. Distinctly on the make."

"In what way?"

"I think she is using Mrs. Blaine's social position and professional fame to push herself."

"Does Mrs. Blaine realize this?"

"Undoubtedly, Captain. Mrs. Blaine is nobody's fool."

"Why would she let herself be used like that?"

"From small snatches of conversation—at dinner and the like—I gathered that Mrs. Blaine has a special reason for befriending Miss Neves."

"What was that, do you know?"

"Mrs. Blaine is making a study of her, for literary purposes. From what I happen to have picked up, Mrs. Blaine intends writing a play about her."

"How about Miss Neves and *Mr*. Blaine?"

"Nothing sir. But then, even if she—ah—had ideas about him, she is much too smart to show it."

"And Mr. Blaine?"

"Oh, no, sir. He has no eyes for anyone but his wife."

"Well, Austin, that's all for the present. If you will wake Mrs. Blaine and tell her I wish to see her—"

"But, Captain! At this hour? It must be something very serious—"

"It is. Do as I say. And don't drop any hints. I'll do all the talking."

"Yes, Captain."

Austin led the way up the stairs, Croy right on his heels.

CHAPTER XXVII

Croy's first ring at the door roused Myra from the fitful doze which exhaustion and the sleeping tablets had induced. Her ankle throbbed with pain, but it was duller now, and if she lay perfectly still, almost bearable. She lay, awaiting the climax to the grisly drama she had projected. She knew it must be the police at the door, after all this time. She had half expected Irma to rush over here immediately after finding Lester's body, but that would have been hours ago. This could only be the police. She braced herself for this final scene. If she got through it creditably, she had nothing to fear and her plan would have succeeded completely.

She strained her ears but could hear nothing from below. When a full ten minutes passed, it came to her that the police were questioning Austin before rousing her. She turned over in her mind what Austin could vouchsafe that could help or harm her. She knew that Lester had never swerved in public—or in private, either, for that matter—in his attitude of devotion to her. If he had fooled her as thoroughly as he had, he must certainly have fooled the servants, too. But considering his hungry passion for Irma, it was possible that the mask had slipped at some moment when he and the girl were alone together, and Austin might have seen it. It bothered her out of all proportion. She could not brook the world to have the slightest hint that Lester had strayed. Her self-esteem demanded that he had died the completely adoring husband.

At last, Austin's discreet knock sounded. She let him knock twice and then answered sleepily, "Come in."

Austin opened the door as she pulled on the dim bed light.

"I regret exceedingly, madame—" he began.

"What is it, Austin?"

"The—someone from the police is here, madame—"

Austin was gently set aside, and Croy appeared in the doorway.

"Mrs. Blaine, I'm sorry to disturb you like this—"

"Something's happened to Irma!" she exclaimed.

Croy closed the door with Austin on the outside.

"May I come in?" he asked superfluously.

"Yes. What's wrong?"

Croy took his time. He introduced himself and with her impatient permission, took the chair at her bedside. He compared her drawn and tired face to the handsome dead face of the murdered man and wondered what bond had drawn the two so close as to be a byword with all the people he had interviewed.

"Mrs. Blaine, why do you think something has happened to Irma—that would be Miss Neves, I take it?"

"She sounded so frightened when she phoned."

"*Phoned?*"

"Yes."

"When was that?"

"About twelve."

"Can you be more definite?"

"No—I didn't really notice to the minute."

"Would you say it was before or after twelve?"

"Before if anything. Perhaps five of twelve."

"What did she say?"

"She asked Mr. Blaine to come over as fast as he could—it was urgent—I don't know her exact words. My husband will tell you."

"And he went?"

"Immediately. I was worried."

"Then he was dressed? Not in bed yet?"

"Oh, no. He was reading aloud to me—we were waiting for the sleeping tablets to take effect."

"You had taken sleeping tablets?"

"Oh—of course, you don't know. I had hurt my ankle rather badly earlier in the evening. Mr. Blaine was afraid I'd have a bad night so he gave me some tablets. I was beginning to be drowsy when the phone rang. But, Captain Croy, what has happened?"

"In a moment, Mrs. Blaine. First I want you to tell me everything you can about that phone call."

"Ask my husband. He took it, he can tell you exactly."

"I want your version, too, please."

"I can tell you what Les said to her at this end but—"

"Do that, Mrs. Blaine."

"Well, he must have said, 'Irma,' because I knew at once who was calling. Then he said, 'You mean *now?*' and then 'What's wrong?' and sometime during the call he said 'Calm down, I can hardly understand you'—as if she were excited or frightened. Finally he said, 'All right, I'll be right over,' and hung up."

"What did he say after he hung up?"

"He said, 'Irma's rattled about something. I'll have to trek over there.'"

"And he left at once?"

"Yes."

"That means he could have been there at, say, ten past twelve?"

"Oh, easily. It's only a block from here. Captain, what's wrong? Please tell me."

Croy shifted uncomfortably.

"I've got some very grave news for you, Mrs. Blaine—" He paused, and his eyes never left her face.

Inwardly, Myra said, *This is it.* Deliberately and surreptitiously, she moved her right foot toward her left one.

"Go on. The truth is better than this uncertainty."

While he answered her, she knocked her right foot against the injured one smartly.

"Mrs. Blaine, your husband went to his death when he left here. He was shot in Miss Neves's apartment a little after twelve."

The pain from the sharp blow was excruciating. The dull throbbing in her ankle became a sword of pure agony. Every drop of blood left her face. She closed her eyes and sagged lower against the pillows.

Croy, watching the paper-white face, was completely convinced he was looking at a woman, stricken by deep shock and utter surprise. Nobody—not the shrewdest criminal on earth—could control the ebb and flow of blood by will power. Croy, an astute and seasoned officer, would have staked his life that the news was indeed news to Myra.

He gave her plenty of time to recover, while he studied her suffering face and the room in which he sat. He checked that the chair he occupied had already been drawn up at the bedside when he came in. He could well believe that Lester Blaine had sat there and read aloud to his wife. He noticed the clock on the mantel but could readily understand that a woman drowsy from sleeping tablets might not necessarily look at it after Irma's phone call. He saw the tablets and the empty drinking glass on the bed table. He marked the luxurious furnishings of the room and compared Myra's plain face to Irma's beauty. He wondered how much the luxury had to do with the dead man's devotion but remembered the sincerity of Steve and Austin, and called himself a cynic for his doubts.

Myra opened her eyes.

"Please—tell me—how could it happen?—Who—"

"He was shot with a gun which Mr. Stephen Thatcher had given to Miss Neves recently."

"But why? You aren't telling me *Irma*—"

"I am afraid so, Mrs. Blaine."

"Oh, God, then he was right—"

"What do you mean?"

"My poor Les—he begged me— Oh, I can't believe it! *I'm* responsible."

"Responsible for what?"

"He told me she was—unpredictable was the way he put it. He asked me to forget it—my play—he said she was dynamite."

"Did he explain why he felt that way?"

"He said she was like a car without brakes, all right on the flat or going upgrade, but watch out for her on a hill."

"Did he call her uninhibited?"

"He may have—I can't remember. But why should she—Are you sure? Oh—Les! *Les!*"

"Mrs. Blaine, it is very late. I need trouble you no further now. If I want more information, I can come back tomorrow."

"No. Please don't leave me alone—wondering—I'd much rather hear everything—I can't sleep."

"But are you up to it?"

"I am not the hysterical sort," she said bleakly. "Perhaps talking is the best thing for me at the moment; it will keep me from thinking."

"Well, then, as far as we can make out, Miss Neves was in love with your husband. In her apartment we found a note to her saying that he wanted no part of her because he happened to be in love with his own wife. It was on Mr. Blaine's stationery, and tomorrow we will check the writing. It is being checked for fingerprints at headquarters now. Evidently this brush-off enraged her to the point of killing him. She phoned him to come over and shot him in a jealous fury, regardless of consequences."

"She admits it?"

"Oh, no. Far from it. She says she was requested by a mysterious message to come to your garage at midnight and wait there for an hour and during that time, someone else shot him."

"Captain! Irma wouldn't say—she has good common sense. She couldn't expect any such tale to be believed."

"She even says she saw your secretary drive into the garage while she was waiting."

"That's impossible. Eve's away. Her car has been in the garage all day."

"She also accused Mr. Thatcher of committing the murder."

"Steve? She must be out of her mind!"

"Nor did she spare you. She advised me to check on your so-called sprained ankle."

"Oh! You mean that *I*—"

"Not I. Miss Neves's idea."

"Well, why don't you check?"

"As a matter of fact, for your own protection I ought to. I'd like to be able to say, of my own knowledge, that it would have been impossible for you to walk to her apartment."

For answer, Myra sat up and turned back the sheet at the bottom of the bed.

Croy drew a horrified breath.

"Good Lord! Mrs. Blaine, that ankle needs attention. It's twice its natural size. You must have knocked it shockingly when you fell!"

"I don't know what I hit against." She replaced the sheet.

"You should have a doctor look at it."

"I will, tomorrow."

"But—if you'll allow me, I know a good bit about first aid—it will feel a lot better, firmly bandaged."

"You are very kind, Captain, but I think, until the swelling goes down, it is better not to confine it."

"It must be very painful."

"When you get a mortal blow, you don't notice a mosquito bite," she said drearily. "If I had only listened—"

"You must get your mind off that, Mrs. Blaine. Nobody with decent instincts could have foreseen such a result."

"Where—is she now?"

"At headquarters." Croy's voice was grim. "Booked on suspicion of murder."

"It's a ghastly nightmare."

"It is, indeed."

"I simply can't believe it of Irma."

"Would you be surprised to hear that in her evening bag along with her lipstick and powder, she was carrying a lethal dose of arsenic?"

"Captain Croy!"

"It is my belief that she intended to slip it in your husband's food or drink at the Griers'."

"Oh! That's really too much. Beyond belief. I—I just can't listen to any more. If you'll excuse me, Captain—"

Croy rose.

"I'm sorry, Mrs. Blaine. I shouldn't have shocked you—you have been so forbearing, so controlled, I forgot what you are going through. Please forgive me."

Myra held out her hand.

"You have been very kind, Captain. It can't be easy for you, either—errands like this, dealing deathblows and—" She gave him a heartbreaking smile.

"Isn't there somebody I can call, to be with you?"

"At this hour?"

"I don't like leaving you alone."

"I'll be all right. Some things are easier to bear alone."

"Can I give you a sedative—another of the sleeping tablets?"

"No. I think not. I'll manage. Please ask Austin to give you a drink or anything you wish—"

"Don't worry about me, Mrs. Blaine. Just get some rest. I'll see you in the morning."

"Yes. Good night, Captain."

Croy went down the stairs and with a word of explanation to Austin, left the house. He joined Harris who was till busy in the garage.

"Any luck?" he asked.

"Plenty of prints, Chief. Some I don't know, some of the dead man, but nary one of the dame, so far. And I'm nearly through."

"I hardly expected it."

"What did she do—fly in without leaving a mark on the doors? She must be nuts to think she can get away with that tale."

"She may *try* to get away with an insanity plea. But not if I know it. There's nothing insane about wrapping a dose of arsenic in a Kleenex for use at a party. And nothing insane about putting that gun back in her closet. Dumb, yes. But sane as you or I."

"Well, that finishes it—not a sign of her prints here, Cap. Did she think you were going to swallow that guff?"

"I have an idea that most people did swallow her—guff. With a face like that, she probably hog-tied every man who ever took one look at her."

"She'll get a jolt this time. Her tough luck it's you on the job—the boy with the chilled-steel eye."

"I like a pretty woman as well as the next man, Harris. But in the line of business, Venus de Milo wouldn't get away with first-degree murder."

CHAPTER XXVIII

After Croy's departure, Myra's nerve gave way. Fiery arrows of pain shot through her whole leg, clutched at her heart, and forced inarticulate moans through her gritted teeth.

Austin, tiptoeing upstairs from a sense of duty, shook his head outside her door and felt an unwonted pang of pity.

For the third successive night, Myra lay, exhausted but sleepless, wracked with pain and in desperate straits. She knew she had convinced Croy completely, both as to her grief and the injury to her ankle. But Edgar Van Roon was another thing entirely. She realized that she needed immediate medical attention but she did not dare let any physician see the cut on her ankle. No sprain or break results in an open wound. Questions would be asked to which she had no believable or innocent answer. Suspicion would be aroused and at this stage, when everything else had gone like clockwork, she did not intend to jeopardize her position, even if she had crushed the anklebone. She would simply have to bear the pain for a few days until the cut healed. Then it would be easy enough to tell Edgar that her fall on the stairs seemed to be more serious than she had first thought it. Meantime, the suffering she could not hide would be interpreted as grief for Lester's death.

The morning brought Alice Grier and Lotta Mason posthaste. Steve Thatcher had phoned them both before nine o'clock. Myra refused to see anyone. It was her best defense. Both women remained at the house, eager to be of use.

This simplified matters for Croy, who reappeared at the Sutton Place house at ten. He interviewed them with a view to any sidelights they might throw on the relations between Irma and the Blaines. The women were unanimous that the Blaine marriage was an ideal one, and that Lester had never strayed in thought or action, either with Irma or any other woman.

"He had plenty of chances," Alice vouchsafed. "He was so extraordinarily handsome. Several of Myra's friends lost their heads and stalked him shamelessly. He didn't give them a second look, he simply wasn't interested."

"We all had our doubts at first," Lotta pronounced. "We never thought such a strange alliance could last, but we have all had to admit that, in spite of everything, they were completely happy. Poor Myra is devastated, and I don't wonder."

About Irma they were less in accord. Alice refused to believe Croy's story of the murder and even defended the girl, until she heard about the packet of arsenic in Irma's bag. When she realized that Irma had actually intended to use *her* food, *her* drink, and *her* home, to execute a murder, her soft pretty features hardened with offended resentment.

Lotta's comment was, "I always detested the creature. There was something meretricious and tawdry about her, with all her looks. And something untamed, too. She seemed capable of anything—anything at all. If it weren't so tragic, so heartbreaking for Myra, one would almost say it serves her right for taking up such riffraff." This was Lotta Mason, whose husband owned a powerful chain of newspapers. Her attitude, subtly inculcated in her husband, was to have strong influence on the tone of the press. Before the week was out, Irma was tried and convicted by nearly every newspaper in the country. The Hell-hath-no-fury murder, as it came to be known, was a novelty in the way of a triangle. From a news point of view, it had everything. All over the country, plain, middle-aged but sterling wives were vindicated by the fidelity of this handsome young Galahad. For once, beauty was flouted, and true worth came into its own. If here and there, a skeptical eyebrow was raised, it never got into print.

The cast of the drama gave it nationwide news value. Myra Blaine, the last of the Hudsons, Myra Hudson, the famous playwright, touched a chord of interest from coast to coast. If she was unattractive and oldish, the other members of the cast made up for it. Bobby-soxers pinned Lester Blaine's perfect features on their walls by the thousands. And Irma's face elevated the story to the heights of glamour. Women by the million stared at her picture with a subconsciously sadistic feeling that there must be something wrong about anyone so superlatively lovely.

It might have been touch and go. One susceptible reporter or one sympathetic sob sister might have turned the tide of public opinion in Irma's favor—or at least have given her the benefit of some doubt. But the Mason chain got in its deadly work early, and the rest followed suit. Besides, all chances of a sympathetic treatment were killed instantaneously, when the news of the arsenic in Irma's bag got out.

Meanwhile, on July fourth, the morning after the murder, Croy was busy. He spent an hour in Lester's bedroom and dressing room, going over his effects, looking for any signs of a well-hidden double life—and found nothing. He pocketed several samples of Lester's writing to take downtown. The fingerprint report was already in. Whether or not the writing of the crumpled note was his, he had unmistakably handled it. His prints were still on it.

Croy interviewed Mrs. Link and Lily Wells, getting only corroborative evidence but nothing new. He asked them if they knew whether or not the garage doors were locked when they left the house the night before. Mrs. Link, monopolizing the limelight, answered for them both.

"That wasn't our business. Our work is in the house."

And if Lily's face went from ecru to ivory for an instant, it was not too surprising that Croy missed it. He was, after all, just checking on one minor detail of Irma's tale, and these two were out of the house before even the accident to Myra's ankle. He wasn't expecting any startling evidence from either of them.

In fairness to Lily, it must be pointed out that she was pretty and a good worker, but far from bright, in a deductive sense. It never occurred to her that by keeping mum about "borrowing" Eve's Ford, she was depriving Irma of a lifesaving alibi. She hated Irma, she had not forgotten that Irma had accused her of theft, and she would never have willingly done her a favor. But if, during the weeks that followed, any one had put it to her directly—"Was it you and Alvin Jones who drove the Ford into the garage at twelve-fifty on July fourth?" she would have confessed it, job or no job. But the tabloids which Lily read merely stated that Irma swore that *Eve Taylor* had driven in, and when it was proved by a hundred people that at the moment Eve was dancing at the country club in Southampton, the papers dropped it, and Lily thought no more about it. If Steve Thatcher had been defending Irma, it is possible that he might have ferreted out this vital bit of testimony. But when he left Irma's apartment after her virulent accusation of him, he saw no more of her. With her limited means, the tide of public opinion against her, and her ignorance of the proper type of lawyer to engage, her case was not in the most capable hands. She had the added handicap of being defended by a man who disbelieved her story from start to finish and took the case merely for its publicity value.

At the moment that Croy was interviewing Alice and Lotta, Steve Thatcher was trying without success to reach Miles Street by telephone. Miles, his parents, and Eve Taylor had decided on an extemporaneous picnic and had gone off in the car early in the morning and could not be located. Steve, after leaving an urgent message with the Streets' butler, went around to Myra's to see if he could be of use. He met Edgar Van Roon on the doorstep. Edgar had heard the news on the radio and had rushed over with the same idea in mind.

While Croy examined the contents of Lester's rooms, the two men joined Alice and Lotta in the living room. Edgar had heard only the bare news of the murder, and the other three gave him a full account of the grisly details. Edgar was shocked to the heart. He made a move to go up to Myra.

"It's absolutely no use," Alice told him. "She won't even see us."

"She'll see me," he said firmly. "She can't be left to mull over this ghastly thing alone."

But no amount of pleading, no message sent up by Lily, changed Myra's resolve. The only person she would allow in her room was Lily, and then only for the barest service of bringing her coffee or a basin of water to wash her face. She sent down word that if her friends really wished to help her, they could do so by receiving anyone who came to the house, thus relieving her of the burden of meeting people at a time when she was in no condition to face anyone.

The four arranged to divide the next few days into relays, so that some one of them was always at the house. Lotta took it upon herself to superintend the servants and interviewed Austin and Mrs. Link to that end. Both cook and butler were sweating at the end of the interview and secretly congratulated themselves on being employed by a playwright and not a female dragon. Until Miles could be reached and arrive from Southampton, either Steve or Edgar would be at hand, so that there was a man in the house to handle reporters, police, and other unwelcome bell ringers. They talked in desultory spurts, turning over the various angles of the case. Only once did Steve manage to raise a faint grin among them.

"I phoned to Harlan James," he said. "I thought it only decent to give the poor rabbit warning. He positively squeaked at the phone and asked if it was likely that the police would publish any letters they might find in her desk. When I said I thought they might, the squeak went up an octave. For a gag, I asked him if he didn't think he ought to get in touch with Irma so she'd know she had a friend behind her. The squeak struck high C, and he stuttered something about an urgent business trip. I bet he made Boston in two hours flat."

For Myra, the hours crept like weighted freight trains. She was emotionally drained, her nerves twitching with the reaction from the tension of the past seventy-two hours, her body racked with pain that never for one instant ceased or abated. She was hot and unbathed, the sight of food nauseated her, and in spite of being exhausted to the point of swooning, the constant pulse of fire that beat in her foot and echoed in her heart, kept her from sleep. Twice during the day, she swallowed more of her tablets and dozed fitfully, only to start up, her mouth dry, her head pounding, and her hands trembling. She longed for Edgar's gentle, expert ministrations, the way a thirsty man hankers for water. But through all her misery, one tiny spark of will power kept her from admitting him. Her plan had succeeded in every particular. Lester was dead; Irma was in jail, facing restraints and indignities more galling to her than a quick death; no trace of suspicion attached to Myra; and nobody could point the finger at her as a deserted wife. If the price for all this was a few days of dreadful pain, she would meet the price.

Myra had evaluated the situation perfectly. She could not have contrived a worse punishment for Irma by torture or the rack. The taste of "high life" which the girl had enjoyed for a month through Myra's favor, made the prison cell more odious, more humiliating than if she had never experienced the suavities of living. She had the bitterness of discovering that the emotional spell she had woven about Steve and Harlan James was as if it had never been. She had used the regulation permission for one phone call, to get in touch with James, certain of her power over him and his willingness to help. But Steve had been before her. She received a curt message that Mr. James had left town for an indefinite period, address unknown. These damned clannish insiders, she thought, hung together in a crisis and anyone beyond the pale was thrown to the wolves without a backward glance.

What outraged her most was the knowledge of her own innocence. No matter what plans of murder, cold-blooded and merciless, she had had in mind, she was guiltless of this particular crime. The intricacies of the plot against her smothered her like some strange cobweb, invisible but impenetrable. Whichever way she turned she was enmeshed in some strangling fold of the net.

The note, alleged to have been written by Lester, she knew for a certainty was counterfeit. Too well she knew Lester's real feelings for her, but she had no scrap of proof to offer. Too, she knew that some other hand than hers had dropped it in her living room to be found by the police. But how could she convince them of this? The note she had found in her compact was another part of the forest of riddles. Had Lester really written it? If not, who else had knowledge of their design to kill Myra? Who knew enough to use the word "poison" in the note? Who had so skillfully got her out of the way for the crucial hour while Lester was being killed and the stage set to throw guilt on Irma? Instinct told her it was Myra, but one fact rose to cloud the issue and divert suspicion—why had Steve forced a gun, *the* gun upon her, so that it should be waiting, hidden and accusing, to point guilt straight at Irma? Who knew she kept it on a shelf in the Sherry candy box? Again, how could she establish that Eve had driven into the garage, when she was known to be a hundred miles away? Was the whole thing a giant organized plot of the "clan," to get rid of Lester, one outsider, and throw the blame on her, another outsider? Had Myra befriended her in the first place, *not* for literary purposes, but solely to make a goat of her?

These questions seethed through her mind, beating at her brain like blows. She was utterly impotent to take action, she had to wait patiently until the indifferent machinery of the law took its slow, technical steps, and patience was not in her. She felt like dashing her head against the bars and screaming in frantic rage. But she controlled herself. She was frightened, filled, for the first time in her life, with uncertainty and the inability to go direct to her objective. She did not know where to turn. All these friends of Myra's were now her enemies. There was no one in her old life at Manhasset who would raise a finger to help her. While she had more money than when she arrived in New York, it was still a paltry sum to finance the legal expense of a murder trial. Myra's revenge was beautifully complete.

CHAPTER XXIX

The only figures in the drama that went through July fourth carefree and happy were Eve Taylor and Miles Street. The picnic, a few miles along the shore from Southampton, was a complete success. The elder Streets were charmed with Eve and put her graciously at ease. After lunch, they tactfully settled down for a nap on a blanket, and the glory of the glorious Fourth reached its climax for Eve and Miles. Miles plunged into a proposal almost before his parents had closed their eyes.

"Eve—Eve darling, tell me—you do care, too."

"Not a bit. But I can't pass up getting your parents for in-laws."

"Damn those kids down the beach. I've got to kiss you."

"Coward! Who cares for a few kids?"

No premonition spoiled the perfect day for them. They swam, they talked, they planned, and later broke the news to Miles's parents. At five o'clock, they straggled into the house, at peace with the world. The butler delivered Steve's message to call him back the moment Miles arrived.

Steve was at home, and gave him the story in detail. When Miles came back into the living room, the other three stopped their light talk abruptly.

"Miles! What's happened?"

"Hell's broken loose."

"Tell us!"

"I don't know where to begin. Eve, throw your stuff together. We're leaving in five minutes."

He helped himself to a stiff whisky and gave them a quick outline of the murder.

By six, they were on their way, the shining joy of their day tarnished by the ugly stain of murder. Through the long hours of the difficult drive on roads choked with holiday cars, they talked quietly, their subdued spirits now and then bubbling over in the gaiety of the incurably happy but, for the most part, trying to make sense out of Steve's lurid recital.

"To me it doesn't jell," said Miles. "Irma couldn't work up enough emotion for any man to kill him and endanger her skin."

"Narcissus type, you think?"

"No. Silas Marner. Wherever she is, there's a smell of money."

"Could she have been blackmailing him?"

"And killed him when the payments stopped? That your idea?"

"It's no good. It doesn't explain the note."

"The note's damn fishy, too. Does it sound to you like Lester?"

"Yes, I think so. I've always believed he had a sort of dependent, adolescent love for Myra."

"There's one good thing about the mess. Steve's fallen out of love as fast as he fell in."

"I hope *you* don't learn quick, mister."

"It took me six years to get out of kindergarten."

When they reached the house, Miles came in with Eve. They were surprised and relieved to find Steve awaiting them. Eve made a move toward the stairs to go up to Myra, but Steve caught her arm.

"No soap. She's not seeing a soul."

"But I must—" began Eve.

"That's what they all said—Alice and Lotta and Edgar. Nobody got through the turnstiles. It's the damnedest thing."

"Well, I'm going to try."

"You'll only disturb that pretty little high yaller Lily, who needs her sleep. She's been on the job a full working-day and overtime. She's the only one Myra lets past the door. Lily comes down with bulletins. 'Miz Blaine et some soup.' 'Miz Blaine ast for an ice bag.' 'Miz Blaine had a cuppa cawfee.' 'Miz Blaine moanin' low.' Period. I'm sleeping here tonight. Edgar takes over tomorrow night. Alice and Lotta handle the day crowds. The house has been overrun. Everybody from the upper ten and the Hollywood sultans down to the cops and the tabloids. But nobody sees Myra."

"She'll have to see me," said Miles. "About funeral arrangements and so on."

"That's what *you* think. I sent up word you were on your way in. Our *café au lait* go-between came down with a message to be delivered on arrival; you are to make all arrangements as you see fit. And you are to draw up the endowment of the literary colony at Rhinebeck tomorrow instead of Monday. What the devil does that mean?"

"Myra had the idea of leaving her money to create a foundation for poor but talented young authors," Miles explained.

"And it can't wait till Monday? She sounds like she's afraid somebody's gunning for her as well as for poor Blaine. Didn't anyone tell her the Delilah of Fifty-Seventh Street is in the clink?" There was an undercurrent of sheepish self-abasement in Steve's flippant tone. He was, as Miles had said, thoroughly out of love, but raw with shame at having been so closely in the toils.

"I don't like the sound of the whole business," Miles said. "Myra's levelheaded, as a rule. No matter how deep this goes, I'd have expected her to stiffen her upper lip and carry on."

"Well, actually, she can't get around, you know. Her ankle's still bad."

"That wouldn't keep her from seeing her friends upstairs," Eve pointed out. "But I can understand it. Her feeling for Lester was deeper than anyone realized. And she's always hated showing emotion. She's the most reticent person I ever knew."

"That's Myra, all right," Steve agreed.

"About the gun," Miles asked. "How come you bobbed up with it just when it could do the most harm?"

"My God, Miles, are you trying to read me in as an accessory?"

"Don't be an ass. But it's all so damn pat."

"Not a bit. I gave her the gun because I felt a kind of responsibility for her. I got her that ground-floor apartment and I thought a girl living alone might—hell, what did it matter? If she hadn't had a gun, it would have been the poison or a carving knife or a sock on the bean. Lester's number was up."

"Well—we could talk all night and get nowhere. Eve's tired. Can I take over for you the rest of the night, Steve?"

"No thanks. The living room couch is comfortable, and I may as well see the dogwatch through. You'll get your turn. From the look of you both, you've had an emotional day on your own hook. Do I congratulate?"

"You congratulate *me*," Miles grinned. "Eve needs some of your hardheaded advice. She's got the fool idea I'm nice enough to marry. I'll leave you to it. Good night."

July fifth was a repetition of the day before, only more so. The house was thronged with sympathetic friends and news-hungry reporters. Myra's cohorts handled them all efficiently.

In Myra's room, things moved to a climax. The apathy of the day before gave place to a strange vague Never-Never Land where the gateway between reality and dreams was a veil through which Myra passed back and forth with the ease of Alice in Wonderland. There were hours when the familiar agony caught her in a vise that required all her will power to bear without screaming. There were other hours when everything—memory, emotion, even pain—disappeared, and Myra floated in a light, delicious element where nothing was real except the soft waves of cotton that broke over her and wrapped her round.

During these exquisite periods, Myra babbled without knowing she had uttered a word. But some sentinel, deep in her subconscious mind, kept her from dropping any hint about the last three gruesome days.

By evening, the times of pain and awareness lessened and the spells of blessed relief came oftener and stayed longer. Myra's gray face was no longer gray. It was flushed with a color that gave her dull eyes brightness.

Lily, who had proved faithful and pitying beyond belief, no longer came only when Myra rang. She huddled on a hassock, out of sight but ready for service at the slightest call. She listened to the broken meaningless phrases all day long, frightened but game. But when darkness fell, her superstitious fears grew with the shadows. And when, toward nine at night, Myra suddenly broke into a gay, chuckling laugh, the girl fled down the stairs as if the devil was after her.

Edgar Van Roon, on duty for the night, was reading in the living room. At sight of the terror-struck girl, he started up.

"She laughin'," Lily moaned. "Can't stan' no more dat jabber-jabber. Her sure-nuff crazy, somebody put de eye on her—" All her veneer dropped away. Only the panic remained.

Edgar was up the stairs before Lily's words had ceased, and into Myra's room. Whether the sight of him re-orientated her or whether it was the moment for one of her returns to storm-tossed sanity, Myra was suddenly conscious and in her right mind. Her voice was faint, but she was the old Myra, firmly in charge of the situation.

"I'm glad you're here," she said without greeting. "I need you badly."

"Myra, Myra darling—"

"My poor Eddie! You've had a rough time with me always, haven't you?" She achieved a travesty of a smile.

"Not too bad, dear. I've always been free to see you and serve you."

"I need service now, my friend."

"That's why I'm here."

"Yes. But something besides doctoring."

"Anything, Myra. Everything."

"Good. What I want is a promise."

"You've got it."

"It mightn't be easy."

"I told you—anything."

"It's this. Whatever you see, whatever you surmise, keep to yourself. Ask no questions."

"That's very easy."

"Thanks, Edgar. Fix up my ankle. It hurts damnably. And give me something to make me sleep. But no questions."

"Right."

He uncovered her leg and nearly caved in. From knee to toe, the angry swollen red of erysipelas flared its danger signal. With a word of explanation, he rushed downstairs and returned with his medical bag. Before he even glanced at the ankle itself, he gave her an enormous injection of penicillin.

Then, with infinite care, he turned the foot until the cut, inflamed and virulent, came into view. Without calling Lily, he went to the kitchen and boiled a huge kettle of water. While the water cooled sufficiently for him to cleanse the wound, he busied himself with making her more comfortable. He gave her a hypodermic, and when her breathing relaxed with blessed analgesia, he got to work.

With delicate probe and cotton, he skillfully washed and sterilized the wound. He had never seen one so filthy. On the cotton swabs he found bits of lint, rug fibers, and, to his utter amazement, tiny chips of blue paint. He stared from these last to Myra's now immobile face. He remembered her dictum of no questions and deliberately ordered his mind to refrain from deductions. He wound a loose protective bandage about the cut to keep it sterile, covered Myra, and sat down to spend the night on watch.

By morning, he knew that she was one of the few who do not react to penicillin. Her temperature was astronomically high, her breathing shallow and hurried. The deadly flush of erysipelas now spread above the knee. He used the latest weapon of the scientists' arsenal, the "wonder drug," streptomycin.

He waited.

At four o'clock Sunday afternoon, she suddenly opened her eyes.

"Miles," she muttered.

"Yes, dear. I'll get him."

For the first moment in nineteen hours, he left her bedside. Luckily, Miles was in the house. He had come in the morning with Myra's will and had stayed to reassure Eve who was shocked and frightened at the story Lily told.

At sight of Edgar's drawn face, Miles and Eve stared, afraid to ask their question.

"She wants you," he told Miles curtly.

"I know. She wanted a new will in a hurry. Surely, hurry can't be so—necessary?"

"If she's to sign it—yes," he replied gruffly.

"Good God! Edgar! She was always so strong—" Not a muscle of Edgar's grim face changed.

"She's had a bad heart for the last year," he said stonily. "She wouldn't let anyone know."

Myra got the will signed by a superhuman effort. Austin and Mrs. Link, hastily summoned, witnessed it. At a sign from Edgar, they left the room at once. Myra turned to Eve, a look of urgency in her dull eyes.

"Eve—cylinders—" The heavy eyes fell. She did not speak again.

An hour later she died.

CHAPTER XXX

The week that followed was frenzied for Eve. From morning till night, she was up to her ears in work. There were thousands of letters to answer, hundreds of phone calls to take, scores of wires to deal with. Miles was at the house nearly continuously, making the final decisions in professional and financial matters. There were smudges under Eve's gray eyes, and Miles wondered if she would ever smile again.

By July fifteenth, they had cleaned up the work between them. Eve spent the day packing, making ready to leave the Sutton Place house for good. She was glad to be escaping from the bleak atmosphere of the house, which was no house but only a shell without Myra. The empty rooms chilled her in spite of the heat, and she had an emotional revulsion of feeling as she went from room to room. She reproached herself unduly for her lack of devotion to Myra as a woman. She had always been repelled by a coldness in Myra's make-up. And Myra had refuted it by consideration and generosity—she had left Eve twenty-five thousand dollars and a string of small real pearls.

For Myra, the playwright, she had grieved deeply and genuinely. Perhaps a true artist concentrated all his feelings on his art and so had little left for human contacts. That could explain Myra's coldness. For unquestionably, her work came first with her. Even on her deathbed, her last words concerned her work.

Suddenly Eve's eyes widened at a totally new thought. How could she have been so stupid as not to take Myra's meaning? Of course! Work first! "Cylinders." An intelligent secretary should have known at once. But Eve had been so shocked, and so rushed with small carping duties, she had never really had a chance to interpret Myra's last word. There was good work on the cylinders in the study, which Myra did not want lost to the world. An artist to the last.

She sped down to the study. Sure enough, there were seven full cylinders in the trough. As a rule, Eve took them up to her own workroom and transcribed them, using headphones. But today her apparatus was packed. She would have to use the playback in the study. She found a notebook and pencil, put the cylinders on the spindle and prepared to take down Myra's lines in shorthand as they came from the machine.

But the first sound of Myra's voice unnerved her. The husky well-remembered tones pulled at her heartstrings. Tears blinded her, and her pencil dropped unheeded in her lap. She listened. Then, slowly, the sense of the records came through to her. As an incipient writer herself, she recognized the diamond-clear brilliance of the scene she listened to. Myra had torn the veil of beauty from Irma and revealed the cool and ruthless Moloch who would ride roughshod over armies to gain her ends. She had utilized Miles's suggestion to deprive Irma of her beauty and had made her more potent without it than with it. Eve sat spellbound as the lines poured out.

When the door of the study opened, she started up. Miles and

Edgar came into the room. With a quick movement, she clicked off the switch and turned, still under the enchantment of Myra's magic, the tears still staining her cheeks. But Edgar had heard a phrase or two and recognized the voice. His jaws clamped shut at the sudden unexpected sound.

Eve said, "I'm—just going over her last work. She wanted it saved. I see why. It's the greatest she's ever done."

She wiped her eyes frankly.

"Another time, Eve," said Miles. "I need you now. One last job before you leave. The Parke-Bernet people are here to inventory the house. We're going round with them. Do you mind coming, too, and taking notes?"

"I'll be glad to."

"Then come along. They're waiting. Ready, Edgar?"

Miles had phoned Edgar, as co-executor with himself, to meet him at the house.

Edgar cleared his throat.

"You two go ahead and start without me," he said.

"Oh, I think you—" Miles began.

But Eve, her heart contracting with pity at what she saw in Edgar's face, hustled Miles to the door. Then she darted back to Edgar and said quickly, "I'll put them all back on again. This is the switch."

She was gone, closing the door behind her.

He turned on the switch and sank into Eve's chair, his hand across his eyes.

Again the scene, full of vitality, played itself out. Edgar hardly heard. He was listening only to the voice itself, catching its familiar and heart-twisting cadences. His pain was nearly unbearable, but he could not get enough of the well-loved accents. His thoughts went down the long years, back to their childhood days, to the homely, dynamic, fascinating little girl who had enslaved him at seven, and had never since let go the bonds. From then till now, there had never been a moment when she had not been first in his heart and mind.

His head went up in sharp surprise. It was no longer Myra's voice that was coming from the machine, but two others, both familiar. It took him a moment or two to place them. With a frown of puzzlement, he leaned forward, listening now, intently.

He heard the sordid greedy tale of Lester's ignoble passion, of Irma's lust for money; the thinly veiled admission that she had murdered her father; the evil suggestion to kill Myra; and the hair-raising matter-of-factness with which they weighed the best possible method of slaughter.

When the last cylinder slid into the trough, the sweat was pouring down Edgar's face. He was breathing like a runner. He stared at the little cylinders in the trough as if they were rattlesnakes.

Deliberately he wiped his forehead and forced himself to relax. This thing required thinking out.

He leaned back and marshaled his facts. Lester was *not* the faithful husband who had written a note repulsing Irma's advances. And Myra knew it. She had heard these records, made unconsciously by the two traitors, just as he himself had. Then, if Lester had not written the note found by Captain Croy in Irma's living room, someone else had. But experts had pronounced it Lester's writing, and it bore his fingerprints. Could Lester have been *induced* to write it, as a joke, as a dare, as an unwitting pawn in a deadly game? Very easily, Edgar decided.

If one note could be faked and planted, why not two? It was Irma's misfortune that she had destroyed the note she swore she found in her compact. She could well have been in the garage for the critical hour. With his knowledge of the records, Edgar could surmise why she went so willingly. Bait had been held out that her presence in the garage was necessary to the consummation of the "innocent accident" by which Myra would be eliminated.

Who besides Myra could have known of the menace that hung over her? Who but Myra could have managed to get Lester to write the note? Who else had the twin incentives of fear of death and consuming revenge to drive her?

But Myra had sprained her ankle, she was *hors de combat*, unable to get to Irma's. Edgar thought of the dirt, the rug fibers, the chips of blue paint in the cut on Myra's ankle. He thought of her urgent request for no questions, her refusal to see a physician until she was in pain past human bearing. With Lester dead in Irma's apartment at midnight, Myra was alone in her house for hours before the police arrived. And the indomitable Myra he had known for thirty-five years was fully capable of effecting an injury if it served her purpose. Edgar was no fool. He knew Myra through and through and loved her, not blindly, but in spite of her faults. His mouth twisted with pity; he understood only too well the dreadful irony of the situation. The only place she had slipped up was in miscalculating the self-inflicted damage. It had cost her her life.

He reversed the shield. Lester was a potential murderer. Well, he was dead, had paid the price of his cheap villainy. Lester was no problem. But Irma was indicted for first-degree murder and, as things looked, had not a chance in the world to escape conviction. If the cylinders were produced in court, they would confuse the issue and create doubt enough, possibly, to save her. In Edgar's opinion, she was not worth saving. She was, indeed, about as vicious a creature as one meets in a lifetime. But was his personal opinion grounds for suppressing evidence? He loathed her for her essential evil and for the tragic pass to which she had brought Myra. But his hatred, said his conscience, did not vest him with the power of life or death over any living being.

He recalled a dinner at Myra's well over a year ago, the occasion of his first meeting with Lester. Steve Thatcher had told how a client of his had been acquitted of murder, not because he was innocent, but because vital evidence had been withheld in order to save the reputations of two senators and a billionaire. Eve had exclaimed, "And you call that justice!"

And Lester had replied, "The gal was dead, anyway. Why ruin important people?"

Edgar, scrupulous, honorable, idealistic, had been shocked at the cynicism of Lester's remark. Now, where it was Myra who was concerned, he trained the spotlight on his principles. If he turned in this new evidence, Myra would be branded as a deserted wife, as a murderess, as a monster taking a hideous revenge. She would become a laughingstock and at the same time a figure of horror to the world which now honored her name and paid tribute to her talent.

He thought again of the homely, fascinating little girl who had lived in his heart for thirty-five years. To a man of Edgar's caliber, the struggle between his conscience and his desire to shield the memory of the woman he loved, was far more poignant than it would have been to most men. The sweat streamed down his face. The muscles of his jaws clamped into hard knots. His lips flattened into a grim line. After a long time, he rose, took the last three cylinders out of the trough, wrapped them in his handkerchief, and left the house. His car stood at the curb. He went toward it and then decided against it; the subway was the quickest way to the district attorney's office.

A few hours earlier, Walter Fowler, Irma's lawyer, was conferring with his client. They sat at a table in the visitors' room. Fowler, with false cheeriness, inquired after her comfort.

"Now just say the word and I'll get you anything you want—cigarettes, books, toilet articles from your home—"

"I've got everything I need. What I want of you is to get me out of this."

"Ah! Yes. Well. Now that's something that needs a good bit of doing. As things stand—" He shrugged.

"If you go into it with a defeatist attitude like that, we're beaten before we start," she demurred.

"If we're beaten," he returned stiffly, "it is not because of my attitude." He leaned across the table and went on earnestly. "Miss Neves, I want to help you. The only way I can do that is to know the truth. Again I ask you to be frank with me."

"I have been. I've told you the truth from start to finish."

"The whole truth?"

"The whole truth," she repeated hardily. But her eyes dropped before the disbelief in his.

"You leave me nothing to work with," he said.

"Can I help it? I swear I never *saw* that note till Croy found it."

"Ah, yes, the note. From Blaine. Repudiating you. Giving you a motive for murder."

"That note was never written by Lester."

"The writing is his, and the prints are his. That is established."

"Well, tell me this, if I did read it, why aren't *my* fingerprints on it?"

"A good question. An intelligent one. And one that occurred to me long ago."

"Well?"

"My dear, it wouldn't take the D.A. two minutes to dispose of it. I can hear him. 'Miss Neves, you were shopping the afternoon of the murder? You wore gloves, of course? I put it to you, Miss Neves, you came home, found the note, and in your eagerness, read it before even removing your gloves. Then, in your anger at its contents, you flung it in a corner—'"

"I never got it, read it, or touched it!"

"I'm just telling you what the D.A. would say."

"My word's as good as his. Why shouldn't they believe me?"

"Because, my dear, the weight of evidence against you is overwhelming."

"The evidence is a lot of lies."

"That is for the jury to decide. Now let us consider what the prosecution has to offer. First, the note, as I said, giving you a motive for murder. Then the gun, with your prints on it, found, *not* beside the body, but what is far more damning, hidden on a shelf in your closet, just where you told the police you kept it. Who else knew you kept it there? Who had access to your apartment to get hold of it and put it back? On your own testimony to Captain Croy—no one."

"Somebody *must* have."

"You're not helping me, Miss Neves. Again I beg you to trust me with the truth."

"The truth is, I didn't shoot him."

Fowler sighed.

"As you like. To go on, in that same closet, a quantity of poison—"

"I explained that."

"But you have *not* explained why you carried enough of the poison in your handbag to kill a dozen people. You were on your way to a party where you expected Blaine to be present. You had just read his note, casting you off. I ask you, what conclusion do you think the jury will draw from that arsenic in your bag?"

"He was shot, not poisoned," Irma said through set lips.

"He wasn't poisoned because his wife's accident prevented him from going to the dinner. Mind you, I'm just telling you what the jury will deduce. So what happens next? Around twelve o'clock he gets an urgent phone call to come to your apartment at once—"

"*I* never phoned."

"Mrs. Blaine states you did."

"I'm telling you I didn't. Why don't you trace the call? Then you'd see."

"Because calls made by dial phones are untraceable."

"I *couldn't* have made it. I was in the garage at twelve."

"Ah, yes, the garage. Where you left not a single fingerprint during an alleged hour's wait. Where you saw Eve Taylor, who was a hundred miles away dancing at a country club. Where nobody has come forward to say they saw you come or go to the garage, although you wore a conspicuous white satin dress."

"Can I help that? It's just my hard luck. That's a very lonesome street."

"Miss Neves, do you really think one single person on the jury is going to believe such a fantastic story? Be realistic. Face facts."

"But what can we do about it?"

"We can change your plea," he returned promptly. "You can plead guilty."

"Why should I, when I didn't do it?"

"Believe me, it's your only chance."

"You mean—"

"I mean that if I go into court with our present defense, I fear the worst." He paused ominously.

"The worst?"

"The very worst."

"You mean—the *chair?*" she whispered.

"I am afraid so."

"They couldn't! They couldn't!" she breathed, through white lips.

"Whereas, if you plead guilty, we have a chance—temporary insanity brought on by Blaine's brutal treatment of you—although I confess the arsenic in your bag is a pretty tall fence to hurdle. Still, life is better than—"

"Life! You mean life *imprisonment?*"

"Yes."

"Me? *Me!* The rest of my life in a *jail?*"

"With good behavior," he said soothingly, "it would probably come to only about fifteen years."

"Only! Only! Do you know what you're saying? I'd be nearly forty—my looks gone—my chances gone. No. *No. NO!*"

"Be advised, Miss Neves—"

"Fifteen years!" She began to shake from head to foot. "Do something! Get me out of this! Find some way—"

"The omelet is made," he said sententiously. "We cannot conjure the eggs back into their shells." He rose, "You know I have your interests at heart. Believe me, our only hope is to plead guilty and make the best of a bad mess. I'll leave you now to think it over alone."

"You mean, the very best I can hope for is fifteen years—years!—behind bars—pried on—bossed—caged—"

"And lucky to get that," he returned dryly, his patience with her stubbornness nearly at an end. "Think it over well, Miss Neves."

Back in her cell, there was a roaring in Irma's head as if she were holding a giant sea shell to her ear. A wave of red rage began to sweep over her. With an immense effort, she fought it down. She had to think. As on the night in the garage when she found herself locked in, a film of ice cooled her blood to a still anger, more deadly than any show of temper. She forced herself to sit down and consider the situation.

She sat, still as a statue, only her eyes alive. She tried to weigh Fowler's arguments, to assess her chances. But reasoning was beyond her. Before her staring eyes, pictures zigzagged across the blank wall of the cell, clouding her mind and striking terror to her senses.

She saw a stone prison yard where travesties of women took exercise like horses in a treadmill; she saw her pink-tiled bathroom and longed passionately for a scented bath; she saw herself lying in a cell bunk, her body cringing away from a blanket alive with vermin; she saw the gracious green loveliness of Belmont Park where she had been the most beautiful thing in that setting of beauty; she saw herself pushed about by stony police matrons and what was worse, handled lecherously by woman-hungry jailors; finally, she saw herself free, after fifteen years had drained away her looks, her luminous skin gray, her pansy-blue eyes, red-lidded and dull, her bright hair dingy, her whole person draggled, unappetizing, a thing to pass in the street without seeing.

For a long time, she sat, staring at the wall,

When Edgar came up the subway steps, the hot July air was strident with the shouts of newsboys.

"Extry! Extry! The Hell-hath-no-fury killer a suicide! Irma Neves opens veins with nail file! Get your paper—"

He read the headlines, the stop-press box on the front page. He drew a deep breath. Then he wrapped the cylinders in the newspaper, laid them in the gutter, and ground them under his heel. As he ran down into the subway again, he had the look of a man reprieved at the ultimate moment.

THE END

Made in the USA
Columbia, SC
08 December 2024